# Blood River

Will Black

A Black Horse Western

ROBERT HALE

ISBN 978-0-7198-2449-4

The Crowood Press
The Stable Block
Crowood Lane
Ramsbury
Marlborough
Wiltshire SN8 2HR

www.bhwesterns.com

Robert Hale is an imprint
of The Crowood Press

Typeset by
Derek Doyle & Associates, Shaw Heath
Printed and bound in Great Britain by
CPI Group (UK) Ltd, Croydon, CR0 4YY

*For Ben and Leah, Scott and Cheryl, Sue.*
*And to my gorgeous grandchildren, Ellie, James,*
*Reuben and the latest one, Grace.*
*With love.*

# Blood River

Gold was becoming harder to find as panners by the hundreds swarmed to any site where even the smallest nugget was found. One mine was still operating north of the Sierra Nevadas. And that was the problem. Transporting the gold down narrow, sandy, and rocky trails, wagons were easy targets for outlaws.

The Pinkerton Agency was charged with the security of a large haul of gold. But they had a daring plan. If it worked, 500 gold bars would make it East. If it failed, all was lost. Unknown to them, the Greeley gang had inside knowledge of their plan and were intent on stealing the gold.

At any cost.

# CHAPTER ONE

Sheriff Brad Morgan sat on his favourite sidewalk rocker and surveyed the peaceful scene of the main street in Indian Bar, a thriving but small town, to the north of Feather River.

There had been several gold strikes to the south of Indian Bar, which was the main reason for the town's survival. Most of the sites were dotted along the Feather River and the wealth it brought to the town had seen it rise from tents and sod-builds, to timber framed buildings that were here to stay.

From the view outside his office, he could see the established businesses that were the mainstay of Indian Bar. Starting at the left, the Palace Hotel, boasting a fine French restaurant – not that Morgan had ever eaten there, his pay would never run to that – but it was a fine hotel, used by the town council for its endless meetings.

Next to the hotel was the small gunsmith, Abe Mortimer; the owner was said to be able to make a gun out of anything he turned his hand to. As well as selling weapons and ammo, he also did repairs and made a good living. The boot and shoe shop was the next building along, again, Morgan had never been in there, except to check the door was locked on his daily rounds.

A side alley separated the next block, where there was a billiard hall on the ground floor, and a lawyer's office above it. Next was Latham's Palace, the busiest place in town. Clay Latham ran a tight ship: his spirits and beer were never watered, the casino as straight as a dye. Now the sheriff had been in there on more than one occasion, not all of which were for business reasons.

Lastly, there stood the National Bank, which doubled as the assay office. Plenty of dollars changed hands in that place, Morgan thought to himself as he dug his old briar pipe out and, knocking it on the rocking chair to rid the bowl of spent tobacco, he proceeded to refill it.

Like everything the sheriff did, it followed a ritual. Striking a Lucifer, he allowed the match to burn down slightly before touching it to the tobacco, suck in the pungent smoke while at the same time, tamping down the burning tobacco with his left thumb to make a better draw, and then adding the flame back.

Satisfied the pipe was perfect, he tossed the match aside, blew smoke out like a steam engine and waved his hand in the air to clear the smoke from his eyes.

He sat contented and watched the day's business unfold as usual.

At nine sharp, the bank's front door was unlocked and ready for business. The bank was followed by the gunsmith and the boot store. The saloon and billiard hall wouldn't open until midday, or when Sam Green, the head barman, was good and ready.

Morgan's gaze lifted to the brilliant, cloudless blue sky and then on to the distant Sierra Nevada mountains, their snow-capped peaks reflecting the already bright sunlight, making the mountain tops shine like torches of white light.

A man could do a lot worse, Morgan thought, than spend his life here.

Womenfolk were already making their way to the general store, or the milliners, for those who could afford to shop for clothes and fancy hats or bolts of cloth, just in from the East, to make their own dresses.

Morgan spent the next fifteen minutes tipping his hat as various folks passed by issuing their everyday comments: 'Gonna be a scorcher,' 'Another nice, sunny day,' 'Too damn hot!'

The same folks, the same comments almost every day. Morgan smiled to himself, it was the life he loved, organized, regimented, but best of all, changeless. He liked the predictability of life in Indian Bar. Surprises, he detested.

So when he saw the two riders walk their horses into town and pull up outside Ma Biggs's rooming house, he was immediately on edge.

Brad Morgan didn't like strangers in his town. They were an unknown factor, unpredictable and likely dangerous.

Morgan pocketed his pipe and stood. He watched the riders dismount and stretch arms and legs, then, pushing their Stetsons back on their head, they surveyed the town.

It seemed to Morgan their gazes lingered a mite longer on the bank than anywhere else. Or was that his imagination?

The two men were powerfully built, both standing over six feet tall. Dressed in white range coats, they eased their aching muscles and hitched their horses to the trough.

At least they take care of their animals, was the thought that crossed Morgan's mind. Still, he better find out who they are.

Morgan heaved himself out of his rocker and stood to his full height of five feet eight inches. A solidly built man, in his early fifties, with eyes the same grey as his hair and, with an aura of authority, he stepped off the boardwalk onto the dry, dusty street, and made his way to the rooming house.

The door was still open. Morgan knew that at any time of the day you could see Ma Biggs sitting in the window knitting, so she would have seen the strangers straightaway and be up, and with the door open, before the men had even knocked.

Morgan took time to look at the two stallions at the water trough. Strong, sturdy beasts they were too and, unless he was very much mistaken, Arabian. He noted the saddle boots were empty, wise men never left their weapons unattended.

Both horses bore Western saddles in good condition, as were the animals themselves. No sweating or flecks of foam to denote a mad gallop into town – or away from somewhere, Morgan thought.

'Help you, mister?' A deep voice almost startled Morgan and he spun round. 'Sorry, Sheriff, didn't see the badge.'

'Howdy, friend, just checking out you newcomers,' Morgan said. 'Staying long?'

'Seems that question must be in a sheriff's handbook someplace!' the man replied, with a wry grin. 'Nope, we're just passing through, staying for a night or two, then on to Sacramento.'

'Morgan's the name, Brad Morgan.' And the sheriff held out his hand.

The man took it. 'Amos Barker, my pard's Joseph Swills.'

It was then that Morgan noticed the low-slung holster and the fancy six-gun butt poking out. 'Cowboys?' he queried.

Amos Barker caught the sheriff looking at his side iron, and a slight grin parted his lips.

'Kinda,' he replied. 'Get whatever work is going.'

'Well, we got a fancy eating place over to the hotel, yonder. French, it is, I ain't never eaten there, not on my wages. An' Ma Biggs is no slouch at cooking, either.'

Amos Barker made no reply, tipped his Stetson at the sheriff and went inside.

Morgan stroked one of the stallions, his mind not at ease. There was more to those fellas than meets the eye, he thought.

He walked back to his rocker, he had a pipe to finish! He sat, puffing contentedly, watching as the two men left Ma Biggs's place and walked their horses to the livery stable. Five minutes later, toting their saddle-bags, the two men walked down Main Street and went into Herb's, the barber.

It was a full hour before the two men emerged, they were hardly recognizable. Hair trimmed and slickered back, clean shaven with fresh shirts and jeans, and boots polished. They look like regular folk, Morgan thought as he watched them walk back to the rooming house.

But he noticed that both men wore their six-guns slung low, and fancy shooting irons they were too; one pearl-handled with fancy silver studs, the other with what looked like a stag handle, and probably a Smith & Wesson.

He was too far away to see any notches.

Amos and Joseph entered their room, a Spartan affair, a wash-stand with a bowl and jug but no soap, a chest of drawers, one of which was missing, a small oil lamp and two single beds.

'You reckon they'll show up?' Amos asked.

'Well, according to the agency snitches, the gang obtained information on the shipment route, so I reckon they will. When's the shipment due in?'

'Midday tomorrow,' Amos said.

'We better check in with the bank manager, make our presence known and what might or might not happen.' Joseph took a deep breath and said, 'But right now I could murder a beer!'

'Bank first, then the beer, OK?' Amos replied.

'OK.'

Sheriff Brad Morgan was on his third pipe of the day as he took in the view he had from his rocker. It had been a morning of howdys, as folk waved or stopped for a brief chat. Morgan was well respected in town both as a decent man and a fair and straight lawman.

Morgan cut short his chat with Abe Mortimer, as he saw the two strangers leave Ma Biggs's place and walk across Main Street to the bank. Abe didn't notice and kept on chunnering, but Morgan didn't hear a word. The sheriff held up his hand to silence Abe and Abe, not the most astute of men except when it came to guns, turned and stared in the direction Morgan was looking.

'Trouble, Brad?' Abe asked.

'Not sure, Abe. Not sure.'

'Them fellas sure don't look like bank robbers,' Abe said, and chuckled.

'Looks can be deceptive,' Morgan said, straight faced. 'I mean, you don't look like no gunsmith, either.'

Morgan stood, intending to walk casually towards the bank. Abe followed.

'You best go about your business, Abe, don't want you caught up in any gunplay,' Morgan advised.

'I might be an old-timer, Brad Morgan, but I can still handle a piece. I'll wait opposite the bank – in case.'

'Just keep that rusty old Remington in your holster,' Morgan said.

'Rusty! What the—'

But Morgan was already halfway across the street. Stepping up onto the boardwalk outside the national bank, Morgan shielded his eyes from the reflected glare of the sun as he peered through one of the windows. Nothing seemed out of the ordinary, there was a queue at the cash desk, but no sign of the two strangers. Puzzled, Morgan pushed open the door and entered the bank. Hank, the hired doorkeep/guard greeted him.

'Everything OK in here, Hank?' the sheriff asked.

'Sure is, Sheriff, OK as it always is.' Hank smiled, showing yellow-stained gappy teeth.

'I noticed two strangers came in here, but I can't see 'em,' Morgan went on.

'That's cos they're in with Mr Morrison,' Hank told him.

'Hmmm.' Morgan rubbed his chin in thought. What the hell were they doing seeing the bank manager? The one called Amos had already told him that they were only in town overnight.

Morgan was about to speak, when a clerk, leaving the manager's office by the staff exit behind the counter, called across to him.

'Sheriff Morgan,' the clerk called out discreetly, and motioned the sheriff over with a crooked finger.

Morgan stared at the fresh-faced youngster. He wore a crisp white shirt with a pencil tie, under a plain black vest. Both arms wore shirt garters as the

14

sleeves were far too long.

'Sheriff Morgan,' the youth cried out again. But still Morgan did not move.

Morgan did not like being beckoned by a whippersnapper, too full of his own importance.

Crooking his own forefinger, Morgan beckoned the youngster over.

The clerk looked aghast at being called over, he shucked his shirtsleeves up, cleared his throat, pulled his vest down and unlocked the connecting door, carefully locking it again behind him, and walked over to the sheriff.

'You want to talk to me, boy, you come over, I don't take too well with crooked fingers. *Comprende?*'

The young clerk looked crestfallen and hung his head on his chest. He was both angry and embarrassed as the sheriff's comments were heard by all in the bank.

'Sorry, Sheriff,' he managed to say, but so softly only the sheriff heard him.

'Now, what was it you wanted, boy?' the sheriff asked.

The word 'boy' obviously rankled, and he showed it on his face. 'Mr Morrison wants to see you, Sheriff. He's in his office.'

'Tell him I'll be right in,' the sheriff answered.

'He said it was urgent, Sheriff.'

'I said, I'll be right in!'

The clerk opened his mouth to say something, but then thought better of it. He turned, with as much bravado as he could manage, walked back across the bank floor and unlocked the connecting door. Closing it behind him, he relocked the door and knocked on the manager's door.

Morrison's booming voice could be heard nearly all over town as he said, 'Come!'

The clerk disappeared inside.

'Sheriff says he'll be right over, Mr Morrison,' he said in a quivering voice.

'Where is he?' Morrison boomed again.

'He's right outside, sir, talking with Hank.'

'Then get him in here—'

At that point there was a sharp rap on the door.

'See who that is,' Morrison said, and the young clerk, easing his collar, opened the main door to the manager's office.

Morgan stepped inside. Although he hid it well, he was surprised to see the two strangers sitting, relaxed and each with a glass of whiskey.

'What is it, Jim?' Morgan wasted no time on small talk.

'Sheriff, I'd like to introduce you to Amos Barker and Joseph Swills; gentlemen, Sheriff Brad Morgan.'

Amos and Joseph stood, ready to shake hands, but Morgan made no effort to move.

Embarrassed, Morrison quickly filled the void.

'Brad, Mr Barker and Mr Swills are Pinkerton men, sent here by the mining company in Sacramento. There's a large gold shipment coming down from the north and it'll be stored here overnight.'

'What the hell for?' was Morgan's first reaction.

'May I explain here, Mr Morrison?' Amos asked.

'Sure, Mr Barker, go right ahead.'

'Sheriff, the mining companies have been increasingly concerned over the security of all gold shipments. In the past month there have been six raids on wagons heading south through the Sierra Nevadas on their way to Sacramento. We estimate that over three million dollars' worth of gold has been stolen.'

Amos Barker paused to let this information set in Morgan's brain. He'd dealt with local sheriffs in the past and knew how some of them took offence at outsiders coming into their territory and ruling the roost. So Amos was at his diplomatic best.

'Obviously we need your help, Sheriff. We're running two heavily armoured Conestogas, specially outfitted for the purpose. One of them has a heavy armed guard, the other has just the driver and shotgun.' Amos paused to see if the sheriff had any questions, when he found he didn't, he went on.

'One of the wagons has six men hidden in the back behind three-inch thick side panels with gun slots. The other has six tonnes of gold on it.'

'Let me guess,' Morgan piped up. 'You're running a dummy wagon as a trap.'

'Exactly, Sheriff. We aim to draw the outlaws into the open and then take them down.'

'How the hell you gonna get wagons over the Sierras? Lightweight wagons find it hard going, with Conestogas—'

'As I said, Sheriff, these wagons are specially prepared. We're not going over the Sierras, we're going

17

*through* them!'

The look on Morgan's face was a picture. '*Through* them?'

'Precisely, Sheriff.' It was Joseph who spoke next. 'We've adapted one of the wagons.'

'Adapted how?' Morgan asked.

Barker and Swills looked at each other before Amos took up the reins again.

'An army engineer designed a wagon that would sail down the river,' Amos began. 'It's been specially fitted out and caulked and, once the wheels are discarded, the wagon becomes a boat!'

'That's the most ridiculous idea I ever did hear,' Morgan snapped. 'You're taking six tonnes of gold down the Feather?'

'Then on to the Sacramento river,' Joseph added.

'That's got disaster written all over it,' Morgan said, sourly.

'It's been well tested, Sheriff,' Joseph said, irritably.

'And how do you know there's gonna be a raid?' Morgan asked.

'Our intelligence has pointed to one gang. The Greeley gang.'

'Never heard of 'em.' Morgan was dismissive.

'Why would you, Sheriff? They operate mainly out of Nevada and much further to the south. The only clue that we have is that their leader, Jed Greeley, rides a grey.' Joseph stopped talking and looked at Amos.

'No witnesses?' Morgan asked.

'Sure, plenty of witnesses, but the gang wore hoods, all we know is that there are five of them,' Amos said.

'So where do I fit into this scheme?'

'The decoy wagon is spending one night in Indian Bar. The Conestoga has also been adapted so it will float. All we need is an armed guard for the night,' Joseph said.

'Let me get this clear,' Morgan said. 'You want me to get volunteers, deputize them and ask them to risk their lives and stand guard all night on a decoy wagon?'

'Sheriff, for all we know, the Greeley gang could be in town already, just waiting to attack!' Amos was losing patience.

'Mr Swills, there ain't been no strangers in town 'ceptin' you two, an' for all I know you could be in that gang.' Morgan stopped and waited for their reaction.

'Brad,' Morrison said. 'I have in my hand letters of credit for both Mr Swills and Mr Barker from the Pinkerton Agency, plus a signed letter from the governor of California, pledging his support of the operation.'

Morgan studied the letters, but you could see from the expression on his face that he wasn't convinced, but he had to concede defeat.

'They look real enough,' was all Morgan said.

'So, can you get some men together, Sheriff?' Amos asked.

'When is the wagon due in?' Morgan said.

19

'Two days' time,' Amos said, 'should be here by mid afternoon at the latest.'

'If'n you've got six heavily armed men in that wagon, what do you need my men for? Surely the men you already have are capable of guarding the wagon overnight.'

'Sheriff, those men will already have had six days and nights on that wagon in cramped conditions, we thought it best they get at least one night's sleep before setting off for Sacramento,' Amos Barker replied.

Sheriff Morgan had to admit, to himself only, that their explanation made sense, but still he was suspicious. It was all too pat. The answers to his questions rolled off their tongues with ease. But for the moment, he kept quiet.

'And the real gold wagon?' Morgan asked.

Barker and Swills looked at each other before Swills answered.

'That information is classified, Sheriff.'

'Classified, my ass,' Morgan exploded.

'We have orders from headquarters, Sheriff,' Swills added.

'Then I suggest you telegraph headquarters,' Morgan stated. 'Cos if I don't have the whole picture, I do diddly-squat. You got that?'

# CHAPTER TWO

Jed Greeley sat nursing a beer in a small saloon in Poker Flat, just south of Indian Bar. He was waiting for his man to show up with vital information, and Greeley didn't like waiting.

He drained his glass and walked to the rough wooden bar counter, this time ordering a whiskey. He lifted the shot glass and downed the contents in one and ordered another. 'Leave the bottle,' he rasped, his patience beginning to wear thin.

As he took the second shot, he saw the thin, weasely-looking man tentatively enter the saloon. He took half a step inside and the batwing doors thumped into his back, pushing him another step forward.

The man looked sick, his face was a mask of sweat and his eyes seemed to dart in every direction at once. His clothes looked as if he'd been born in them and, even from a distance of some twenty feet, Greeley could smell the rank, sour odour of a man who hadn't washed in weeks.

The gaunt man turned towards Greeley and a look of recognition crossed his sallow face and what appeared to be a grin, showing black teeth highlighted by almost white lips.

The man removed what had once been a high-crowned Stetson and clutched it in both hands as he shuffled forwards.

Greeley picked up his bottle and shot glass, asked for another glass then moved to the far corner of the saloon; he picked a table where he could sit with his back against a wall and from where he could survey the whole room.

He watched as the sorry excuse for a man changed direction and headed towards the table, licking his lips as he saw the almost full bottle of rotgut and a spare glass.

Without waiting to be asked, the man sat down and leered at the bottle.

'Help yourself,' Greeley said, with a look of disgust on his face.

The man's hands were shaking as he dropped his hat on the floor and reached for the bottle, using both hands to pour the contents into the glass.

Greeley had met the man, Jacob Trent, in a Sacramento dive on the day he had been fired from the Pinkerton Agency. The man was a low-life clerk and his habitual drinking had been his downfall.

But Trent had got it into his head that he was being victimized and bore a grudge, a grudge that Greeley, with the aid of free whiskey, had been able to exploit.

The meeting had been purely by chance. Trent had fallen over, drunk as usual, right at Greeley's feet. At first, Greeley ignored the man and was tempted to add to the man's woes by kicking him out of the way, until he saw a headed notepaper that fell from the man's vest pocket.

It was headed The Pinkerton Agency.

Jed Greeley was nothing if not an astute opportunist. Straightaway, his brain was working feverishly to turn this chance meeting into his advantage.

And all it took was a bottle of rotgut and the spare cot in his hotel room.

The following morning, over breakfast, which for Greeley consisted of a mountain of bacon, three eggs, a hunk of fresh bread and coffee, and for Trent, whiskey, Greeley gradually managed to get information from the ex-Pinkerton clerk.

That the man bore a grudge was obvious. And Greeley encouraged him to want to get even. Trent, not the smartest cookie in the box, couldn't see how he could ever get even with such a large company, but Greeley had ideas aplenty, which he soon explained to Trent.

'Reckon I could help you get your own back, Trent,' Greeley said, waving over the waitress and ordering coffee for himself and whiskey for Trent.

Trent licked his lips, more in anticipation of the whiskey than Greeley's offer of help.

'I don't see how—' Trent began.

'You were a clerk at the agency, right?' Greeley asked.

23

'Yeah. . . .'

'So you must have some idea of what was going on there with regard to, let's say, collections and deliveries.'

'Yeah, I had access to the ledgers,' Trent said.

They were silent for a moment as the waitress brought the coffee and whiskey over.

'So, anything unusual stick out?' Greeley asked.

With a shaking hand, Trent picked up the tumbler of whiskey and took a sip. He seemed to relax slightly as the liquid found its way to his empty stomach.

'Well,' Trent said after a long pause. 'There was something going down I didn't get the hang of.'

Greeley waited, impatiently, for Trent to continue. When he didn't, Greeley pushed a little. 'And what was that?'

'Well, we had some strange bills in for two Conestogas,' Trent said, and sipped more whiskey.

Again, Greeley waited for the man to continue, but it seemed he was only capable of one sentence at a time. Losing patience, Greeley said, 'You wanna explain why that's so strange, in more than one sentence?'

'Well,' Trent paused while he took out his makings, 'we got wagons coming out of our ears, and very little storage space left. But these two wagons were in a secure compound, and no one was allowed in, 'cept workmen.'

'And you have no idea why?'

'Nope.'

'Can you find out?'

24

'I have a drinkin' buddy there, I could ask him what he knows,' Trent answered and finished the rest of his whiskey.

'Well, will you do that?' Greeley asked.

'Sure, I'll go see him after he finishes work.'

'Good. I'll meet you in the saloon around eight,' Greeley said and stood, indicating their meeting was over.

Trent was hoping for another drink, but soon saw that was a forlorn hope as he watched Greeley leave the dining room.

'You're late,' Greeley said as Trent downed the shot glass of whiskey in one go.

'Ol' Tom had to work late,' Trent replied matter of factly.

'So?'

Trent stared vacantly at Greeley as if he hadn't a clue what he meant.

'Did you find anything out about the Conestogas?' Greeley added. He was getting mighty tired of this man and wondered how the hell Pinkerton's came to employ him in the first place.

'Yeah, found out some stuff,' Trent said.

Greeley was now angry, his right palm went to his Colt and he had to control himself not to draw and end the life of this miserable low-life.

'Seems them wagons have been caulked and some sort of quick release wheels fitted,' Trent went on. 'Ol' Tom reckons there's gonna be a gold shipment made.'

This news made Greeley more interested and he

25

pushed the whiskey bottle towards Trent.

'Don't mind If'n I do,' Trent said, pouring himself a large measure.

'Any idea of dates and route?' Greeley asked.

'Not yet, but ol' Tom reckons there's something strange going on,' Trent said.

'Strange? In what way?' Greeley said and leaned forward, his interest now intense.

Trent took his time in answering, sipping at the whiskey and seemingly getting his thoughts in order.

'Well, Tom seems to think them there wagons look more like boats than wagons.'

Greeley reached out for the whiskey bottle and poured Trent and himself another shot, his mind racing.

'Tom reckons they aim to move out pretty damn soon as they got themselves a team of men there working all the hour's god sends, an' they're on a bonus and sworn to secrecy.' Trent sank his third whiskey and again smacked his lips.

'When can Tom get that information?' Greeley asked.

'Later tonight. One of the workmen is an old buddy of his an' they're meeting here at around eleven,' Trent said, looking at the bottle again. 'He also said the information would cost.'

'You told him about me?'

'Had to,' Trent replied, 'wouldn't tell me lickety-spit till I told 'im.'

This was an added complication for Greeley.

Now he'd have to kill two men!

# CHAPTER THREE

Sheriff Brad Morgan sat at his desk leafing through his pile of Wanted posters.

He hadn't recognized Barker or Swills, but he wanted to make sure there were no posters out on them.

As he finished the first pile, Bart, the telegraph operator, came in.

'Message for you, Sheriff,' he said, and handed over the handwritten note.

'Goddamn, Bart, looks like a spider's done a jig across the paper.'

'Sorry, Brad, I left my readin' glasses at home and these ones are for picking up a beer pot and dodging horses.' Bart's face broke into a toothy grin.

'So what does it say? Morgan asked.

'Well, from what I can recall, it was from a Mr A. Pink,' Bart said.

'You sure it was Pink, not Pinkerton?' Morgan said.

'Nope. Definitely Pink.'

'What did he say?'

'Just that you were to give every cooperation, and the governor would telegram you later.'

'That all?'

'Yup. Coffee on?'


Outside, on Main Street, the weekly stagecoach pulled up outside Latham's Palace.

Sheriff Morgan stood, and walked to the window where he had a clear view of the stagecoach and, more importantly to him, whoever might get off it.

'Well, I'll be a sonuvver,' Morgan said.

Bart joined him at the window. 'By golly!' was all he could say.

Both men were entranced by the beauty who stepped down daintily from the stagecoach.

Dressed in a long lilac skirt with a matching bolero jacket, white blouse and lilac hat with a white feather, she stood and surveyed the town briefly as the driver and the shotgun removed her luggage from the roof net and carried the suitcases into Latham's Palace.

She raised her parasol, which exactly matched the lilac of her outfit and, lifting her skirt to reveal highly polished black boots, she stepped up onto the board-walk and entered the saloon.

It seemed the whole town came to a standstill as open-mouthed men watched her graceful movements.

'By God! I wish I were twenty years younger,' Morgan said, and sighed.

Bart laughed. 'Sheriff, you'd have to be a thousand times richer too!' Both men grinned.

'Think I'll do my duty and introduce myself,' Morgan said, donning his Stetson before strapping on his ancient Remington and gun belt.

Daisy Rae Mahoney was the talk of California. Not only was she a beautiful woman, she had the voice of an angel. Even the roughest, toughest hard men would be brought near to tears by her singing.

For Clay Latham, this was a major coup. Indian Bar was no great cultural metropolis, that was for sure. With the Sierra Nevada mountain range to the west and south, scrubland to the north, the river was its life-blood, that, and the panners and gold mines, which brought dollars to the town.

It was the dollars that brought Daisy Rae to Latham's Palace. But it was not all paid by Clay Latham.

Amos Barker and Joseph Swills watched as the stage-coach came to a halt outside Latham's Palace.

'She sure is a pretty thing,' Swills remarked, licking his lips.

'She should be, the money she charges,' Barker said, acidly.

'Now that was her manager, I'm sure Miss Daisy isn't—'

'Joe, makes no never-mind. She's here and that's all that matters. When she opens up in two days' time, Latham's Palace will be packed to the rafters. The whole town will be deserted,' Amos said and smiled.

Jed Greeley arranged to meet Trent and his buddy,

Tom, at midnight at an old deserted shack on the outskirts of town.

Trent, looking even more weasel-like, wasn't too happy about the choice of meeting, mainly because there was no chance of a drink.

'We don't want any prying eyes seeing the three of us together,' Jed said when he saw Trent's face drop. 'We don't want folks to put two and two together now, do we?'

'Guess not,' Trent had to agree.

'I'll bring a bottle with me,' Greeley said, knowing this would make Trent feel better about the whole deal.

Trent's face visibly brightened.

It was five hours later when Greeley dismounted at the rear of the shack and tethered his horse to a tree stump.

Entering the dark interior of the cabin, Greeley placed a cheap bottle of red-eye on a rickety wooden table. He wanted to light a lantern, but decided not to, just in case anyone was about.

He checked his Smith & Wesson, adding an extra shell into the breech, making the weapon fully loaded.

His eyes were becoming used to the darkness now. Outside, a full moon lit up the landscape with an eerie blue light, but inside the shack it was pitch black. Just what Greeley wanted. He settled himself in a chair and waited.

It was fifteen minutes later when he heard the soft

pad of hoofs approaching the shack.

Greeley smiled. He just hoped that Trent had the information he needed. They'd die quickly if they had news, but real slow if they didn't!

The horses came to a halt and Trent shouted, 'You in there?'

'I'm here,' Greeley replied. 'So is a bottle.'

Both men dismounted, tethered their animals and entered the shack.

'Sure is dark in here,' Trent said.

'You'll get used to it,' Greeley said. 'Now, what have you found out?'

Pointedly, Trent licked his lips and stared at the bottle on the table.

'Talk first,' Greeley said in a steely voice that brooked no argument.

It was Tom who spoke up.

'Well, sir, Mr Greeley, sir, both Conestogas are finished, but they sure ain't fitted out the same way.'

'Care to explain?' Greeley said, feeling his impatience rising.

'Well, from the outside they look identical, but inside they sure is different.'

'Yeah, I already got that message. In what way are they different?' Greeley was trying hard to keep his temper in check.

'Well, one of 'em has a false floor and there's a whole stack of hay ready to load into it. The other one, well, as far as I could tell, has two rows of seats in the back and under the canvas top there's a wooden wall with what I figure to be slots in it, maybe for a rifle or something.'

'Anything different on the outside?'

'Nope. 'Cept the horses, o' course,' Tom replied.

Greeley gritted his teeth. 'An' how different are they?' he asked in a quiet, but menacing voice.

'Well—'

'Can you start a sentence without saying "well"?' Greeley's lips parted in a sort of smile but his eyes were icy cold.

Tom coughed and thought about that for a minute before answering.

'Er, well, the horse on the false bottom wagon sure is bigger and stronger. Seems like on purpose,' Tom said.

'Like as if they was gonna be pulling a heavier load,' Trent piped up.

'That worth fifty bucks, Mr Greeley?' Tom asked.

'Sure, sure it is. Help yourselves to a drink, boys,' Greeley said and smiled a smile that would damp out a brush fire.

Trent grabbed the bottle and pulled out the cork with his teeth, then took a mighty swig of the contents before wiping his mouth with his filthy cuff and passing the bottle to Tom who grabbed it just as eagerly.

'Boy, that sure tastes good,' Trent said. 'Now about that fifty bucks?'

'Oh yeah.' Greeley smiled. 'Just gettin' my billfold out.'

Greeley's gun was out, hammer cocked, before Trent even realized what was going on.

'Hey, what—'

That was all he managed to say before the Smith & Wesson blasted into his face at almost point-blank range.

The force of the slug catapulted Trent backwards off his chair and sent him crashing into the wall of the shack. The whole building shook as he hit it and for a second, Greeley thought the whole goddamn building would collapse.

Tom had the bottle to his lips as the brilliant flash of the gun almost blinded him temporarily. In shock, he involuntarily spat out the mouthful of whiskey he'd just gulped and the spray hit Jed Greeley in the eyes. It stung like all hell.

Tom saw his chance and, much to Greeley's surprise, moved like an arrow for the door of the shack. He would have made it too, had it not been for one of Trent's legs. Tom tripped over it and went sprawling across the floor.

Jed Greeley, his eyes still stinging, loosed off a shot which caught Tom in the thigh, but still the man crawled on, hoping that he'd make it outside.

Greeley had other ideas.

Clearing one eye with his bandanna, Greeley stood and took aim. The .22 calibre slug caught Tom at the back of the head, slamming his now lifeless body to the rough wooden floor.

Jed Greeley finished wiping his eyes and picked up the whiskey bottle and took a few gulps, not to calm his nerves, but to calm his temper.

Gradually, he pulled himself together and the red

mist began to fade. He took a last gulp of the whiskey and, making sure both men were dead, he left the shack.

Now to get the gang back together.

# CHAPTER FOUR

Sheriff Morgan pushed open the batwings to the Latham Palace and immediately removed his well-worn Stetson.

To his amazement, as he slickered back his sparse, wiry hair, the place was silent.

Not only silent, but every man in the saloon was unmoving, staring open-mouthed at the vision in lilac that had just entered the Palace.

The first man to galvanize himself into action was Clay Latham, who rushed towards Daisy Rae Mahoney with a broad smile on his face. He stopped short of bumping into her – just – and gave an over-the-top bow.

'Welcome, Miss Mahoney, welcome indeed to Latham Palace. I'm Clay Latham, owner, I am delighted to meet you.'

Daisy Rae merely smiled briefly and gave a slight nod of her head. It was a rather stern looking matri-arch, dressed in widows' black who answered Clay.

'Miss Mahoney will go to her room, now. All food

will be taken to her by me. No one is to visit her and when she performs, you will have a minimum of four guards ready to halt any advances made upon her person. Is that clear?'

'Perfectly,' Clay answered, taking an immediate dislike to the woman.

'I have here a list of requirements: fresh flowers must be placed in her room at precisely eleven a.m. at the same time as breakfast is served. Breakfast will consist of freshly squeezed orange juice, toasted bread, jam or marmalade and butter. Coffee must be mild and served with fresh cream—'

'Ma'am,' Clay interrupted, 'had you given notice of your *requirements* I could have organized them for you. This is a gold town, we ain't got no fresh flowers, I ain't even sure we have cream. But I'll find out.'

'I hadn't finished, Mr Latham.' The woman seemed to ignore what Clay had been saying. 'A bath is to be drawn at precisely noon, no additives as we have our own. An armed guard must be stationed outside Miss Mahoney's room at all times. And I mean all times.

'Luncheon will be served at one in the afternoon and will be light. No steak or potatoes, lean ham will suffice and fresh bread and butter. Tea is the preferred drink at this time of day.

'The bed linen will be changed at three in the afternoon ready for Miss Mahoney to take her afternoon nap, which I will supervise. The linen must be cotton and freshly ironed. I have here a written list for your staff so that they know what to prepare.'

She handed over a lilac-coloured sheet of paper.

'I'll see what I can do,' Clay said, 'but I can't promise all this on such short notice.'

'Miss Mahoney will perform from seven in the evening until eight thirty. There will be a fifteen minute interval during which fresh chilled water will be served. At exactly a quarter to nine, Miss Mahoney will again perform until ten. There will be no encores and the guards will escort Miss Mahoney to her room. Is that quite clear, Mr Latham?'

'As clear as the nose on your face, Miss—'

'Mrs, Mrs Mahoney,' the woman answered tersely.

'Mrs Mahoney.'

'Good. We will now go to our rooms.'

Sheriff Brad Morgan watched with interest as the one-way conversation ensued. In all the time what turned out to be Daisy Rae's mother had spouted off her demands, Morgan noticed that Daisy Rae didn't lift her eyes from looking down at the floor once. To Morgan, she looked more than a little embarrassed.

As the entourage, consisting of Mrs Mahoney following Clay Latham, her daughter behind and the stagecoach driver and shotgun carrying their luggage, headed for the stairs, Brad realized he'd missed his chance to introduce himself.

Gradually, men began to talk in hushed tones which, as Daisy Rae disappeared, grew louder and louder and bawdier and bawdier, as men commented on the most beautiful woman any of them had ever seen.

The alcohol-induced banter quickly stopped as the large frame of Clay Latham stomped down the stairs.

He was clearly an angry man.

Without looking or talking to anyone, Latham stormed across the saloon floor to his private table set in the far corner of the large room, a table that had a view of the entire saloon, plonked himself down and snapped his fingers at the barkeep, who immediately knew what was wanted.

Whiskey. Or in this case, fine, single-malt Scotch imported from Scotland at great expense and used only for special occasions – and the barkeep thought this might be one of those occasions.

Brad waited for the barkeep to take the bottle over and then approached the saloon owner.

'Afternoon, Clay. Mind if I join you for a spell?'

Clay Latham grunted and the sheriff took off his hat and sat down. As if by magic, the barkeep returned with another glass.

Latham poured two shots and without waiting, downed his in one.

'If that ain't the most ornery woman I ever did meet,' Latham said.

'She sure rules the roost,' Brad admitted, taking a sip of the excellent whisky.

Latham didn't reply, just poured himself another shot and glowered.

'Well, I can see you ain't in no mood for chit-chat, so I'll be on my way. Got some work to take care of.' Brad drained his glass and stood.

'Sorry, Sheriff. Happen I'll be in a better frame of mind come tonight.' Latham reached into a pocket and pulled out a ticket.

'Here. Complimentary ticket for tonight's show. Be my guest.'

Brad took the ticket. 'Thanks, I look forward to it,' he said and, tipping his hat, he left the saloon.

Back out on the street, Brad's thoughts turned to the recruiting of men he could trust to guard the wagon that was due in the following day.

He still had his doubts about the whole scheme, and he certainly didn't trust Barker and Swills.

Just a gut reaction, but Brad Morgan hadn't lived this long without taking notice of his ample stomach and right now his gut was having one of its reactions!

As he walked back to his office, he saw Barker and Swills cross Main Street and head towards Latham's Palace. Brad stopped and watched as they entered and decided to follow them inside.

He waited by the batwings and saw the two men head straight for the stairs and disappear from sight.

*Now what the hell—*

# CHAPTER FIVE

Jed Greeley had kept his gang together, and avoided their detection by the law, through keeping things simple. After each heist, the gang would immediately split up and wait a month before coming together again to share the bounty at a pre-arranged meeting site.

At first this met with opposition from the gang members; trust took a long while to earn, but after three successful robberies the men began to trust their leader as Greeley turned up with the money they'd stolen and shared it out equally between them – after taking his cut.

Jed Greeley had picked the ambush site with great care. It gave him and his men the high ground while not allowing the stagecoach to leave the trail as it was lined with rocks and boulders that had been cleared to make the trail.

The information that Greeley had paid for, and paid well, was that a payroll was being transported to one of the mining camps and it was travelling with a low profile so as not to attract attention. Greeley had been assured that there was only the driver and shotgun aboard, but that turned out not to be the case.

The gang met with more resistance than they had expected.

Instead of just the one shotgun sitting alongside the driver, there were four more inside. For once, Greeley's groundwork before the robbery proved ineffective. His inside source had fed him false information.

And Greeley cottoned on to it straightaway.

He'd been double-crossed.

Greeley didn't dwell on the matter, he'd settle that score later. Right now he had better things to do.

Taking careful aim, he shot the lead pony, bringing the stagecoach to an abrupt halt. The shotgun sitting next to the driver was tossed like a rag doll through the air to land heavily beside the trail.

The man didn't move.

With the stagecoach halted, the gang peppered it with slugs. The noise was deafening as the hail of death rained down on the hapless guards trapped inside.

The driver threw himself to the ground, unarmed, there was nothing he could do to halt the onslaught and he took cover behind a rock.

At the far side of the stagecoach, the door opened and two men fell out, their bodies riddled with bullets.

Gradually the returning fire from the stagecoach ceased. An eerie silence filled the air, mingling with the black powder smoke and the frightened whinnying of the horses.

41

None of the Greeley gang had uttered a word throughout the massacre. Jed Greeley spat tobacco juice onto the parched ground and edged his horse forward towards the stagecoach, his handgun still drawn.

He peered inside the shattered remains of the stagecoach, riddled with bullet holes and splattered with blood and gore. Satisfied all were dead, he waved his men forward.

'Get the strongbox,' he ordered.

Two men immediately dismounted and went to the rear of the stagecoach. They cut through the netting holding the strongbox and lifted it to the ground and, at a nod from Greeley, one of the men shot the padlock off.

Greeley sat his horse as the two men lifted the lid of the strongbox. One of them whistled. Inside were tight wads of greenbacks and several bags of coins.

One of the men opened a bag and discovered it was full of gold eagles. He took it over to Greeley to show him the contents.

'Share that bag out between the men, it'll keep you in whiskey and women till we meet up to split the rest,' Greeley said.

'Darn right it will,' the man replied, already licking his lips in anticipation.

'Just spend it wisely, don't go splashing it around an' gettin' folks suspicious. You all know the score.' Greeley didn't need the men to reply, they knew the rules.

Wordlessly, the coins and greenbacks were loaded

into Greeley's saddle-bags, he'd take charge of the money for exactly four weeks until the gang met up again, some 200 miles to the east.

Greeley always stashed the proceeds of any crime in the same place. A small cave set high in the Sierra Nevadas where it was safe. He'd leave it there for three weeks, before recovering it and making the 200-mile journey to meet up with the gang.

In those three weeks, he'd plan their next heist.

This time it would be different. Greeley had another task to perform after he'd stashed the money.

No one double-crossed him.


Sheriff Brad Morgan was having no luck in finding any men to guard the wagon that was due in less than twelve hours. It seemed that every single man-jack of them had other plans. It didn't take Brad much figuring to know what those other plans might be: Daisy Rae!

Brad figured, as it was his duty as town sheriff, that he and his deputy would be the only guards available.

He still had doubts rankling him. Too much change in too short a time. And Brad Morgan didn't like change of any sort.

There was something not quite right about this whole situation. Morgan had no proof of any wrongdoing, but a major gold shipment and the visit of a famous singer all on the same day, coupled with the arrival of Barker and Swills, was too much for him to handle.

Back in his office, he filled his pipe, tamped it down and lit up. Clouds of blue smoke filled the room and his young deputy, Clancy Miller, coughed pointedly.

'Ain't no use you coughin',' Morgan said with his pipe clenched firmly in his teeth. 'You better fill that there coffee pot, we got a long night ahead of us.'

'We gonna go see Daisy Rae?' Clancy said excitedly.

'No, we ain't, we got a stagecoach to guard,' Morgan replied.

'What?'

'You heard me, now get that coffee on.'

'But—'

'I don't like it any more'n you do, but there ain't no one else,' Morgan told him.

'What's so special about a wagon?' Clancy asked. 'What's in it?'

'Nothing,' Morgan drawled.

'Nothing? We gotta guard a wagon with nothing in it?' Clancy was steaming up. 'We gotta miss Daisy Rae for *nothing*?'

'We got a job to do and do it we will. Coffee!' Morgan ordered.

Amos Barker and Joseph Swills stood in the corridor outside the rooms of Daisy Rae and her mother/chaperon/manager, and not necessarily in that order. Hats in their hands, Barker knocked three times on the door which opened almost immediately, as if Mrs Mahoney was waiting there.

'Ma'am,' Swills and Barker said simultaneously.

'You got the money?' Mrs Mahoney asked without acknowledging either man.

Swills reached into the inside pocket of his jacket and brought out an envelope. Mrs Mahoney snatched it out of his hand and leafed through the bills inside.

'You counting it?' Barker asked.

Mrs Mahoney didn't answer.

'You sure are an ornery bit—'

'It's all there,' was all she said as she slammed the door shut.

# CHAPTER SIX

The two Conestogas had left the gold camp north-west of Indian bar some three days earlier. The dummy wagon had left a day before the gold-laden wagon. Its speed would naturally be slower; six tonnes of gold was a heavy load and the trail to Indian Bar was no picnic.

Littered with rocks, the winding trail was slow progress and this, coupled with the heat, was something that hadn't been given much thought to by the mining company.

As the first day wore on, the temperature inside the wagon became more and more stifling. The six men, crammed together inside a wood and metal cage with very little ventilation, were beginning to suffer. The conditions inside the wagon were cramped and uncomfortable and the men, their bodies sweating profusely, were struggling to keep alert.

By noon that first day the heat was unbearable and the men inside the wagon were finding it increasingly difficult to breathe.

They had been ordered not to break their cover under any circumstances in case the wagon was being trailed and their cover blown.

'I gotta get out of here,' one of the men said at last. 'I can't breathe!'

'You stay put,' Bert Williams, the boss of security said.

'There ain't enough air in here,' another man piped up

'You're still beathing, ain't ya? Quit your gabbing and save your breath!' Morgan advised.

It was then that a shot rang out.

The heavy .44 slug from the Henry rifle tore into the flanks of the left lead wagon pony, bringing it down instantly.

As the horse fell, it toppled the horse behind it and then the other two horses on the right side of the wagon were overwhelmed as the momentum of the heavy Conestoga took over.

The driver and shotgun were thrown forwards in a high arc to land some thirty feet in front of the wagon.

Their survival was short-lived as both men, stunned, watched as the careening wagon was flipped end over end as the now dead horses were dragged beneath it.

The last sight they had of this world was of tonnes of wood, metal and the bodies of six men crushing them to death.

All done with one .44 slug.

*

As the dust settled, Jed Greeley lit a cheroot and ordered his men to finish off any survivors, convinced as he was this was the dummy wagon.

'What about the gold?' one of his men asked.

'There ain't no gold in *that* wagon,' Greeley replied.

'Then what—'

'The less you know right now, the better,' Greeley cut the man off. 'Now go check that wagon!'

Four men walked their horses down the slope towards the wagon. They dismounted and checked the mangled mess before them.

No further shots were fired.

There was no need.

'That wagon should've been here by now,' Clancy Miller said, feeling more and more frustrated at a wasted night when he could be watching Daisy Rae and whooping it up with the rest of the male inhabitants of Indian Bar.

'Yup,' Sheriff Morgan replied. 'It should.'

'Well?'

'Well what? You want me to snap my fingers and produce it?' Morgan busied himself with his pipe. 'We'll just have to wait for it.'

Clancy let out a long, drawn out sigh. He walked to the office door and stared across Main Street. Latham's Palace was ablaze with light and the din of voices and laughter could be plainly heard. Clearly the place was packed to the rafters.

'Go on, git,' Morgan said. 'If'n I need you I'll

come and get you. Don't drink!'

'Sheriff, you're the best!'

'Yeah, I know.'

Clancy yanked open the office door but before he could leave, Morgan called out, 'You'll need this.' In his hand was a ticket.

Clancy ran across the office, grabbed the ticket and ran back to the door, stopping only briefly to say, 'Thanks, Sheriff.'

'Get outa here,' was all Morgan said, and lit his pipe.

Sheriff Morgan was more concerned than he let on. He hadn't liked the plan from the outset; he didn't trust Barker or Swills but had no proof to back up his suspicions.

He decided that, if the wagon didn't show up, come first light he'd take a ride along the trail and see what the problem was.


Jed Greeley got his men to start clearing the trail of evidence. It was no easy task.

The bodies were unceremoniously dumped in a deep gulley and covered with brush. A temporary measure as buzzards would soon start to gather, wheeling high in the sky waiting for the opportunity to feast on the grisly remains.

The horses were harder to move, but they too were dumped in the gulley and more brush covered them.

Now for the hardest part. The wagon itself. Although some parts were shattered, the main body of the heavy carriage was still in one piece and the attempt at bullet-proofing with the use of iron sheets inside the wooden shell, proved difficult to move.

The noon-day sun was on the wane and the ground began to release its heat, adding to the stifling air which seemed to sear the men's lungs as they toiled, stopping frequently to drink water to ease their parched throats.

After almost three hours, the last remnants of the wagon were thrown into the gulley and the trail was cleared of any signs of the massacre.

Jed Greeley walked up and down the trail looking for any tell-tale signs and, although the dirt was churned up in places, it would take an experienced tracker to spot it – given the trail was well-used.

Satisfied, Greeley and his gang mounted up and headed for their next destination.

Indian Bar.

# CHAPTER SEVEN

The gold-laden wagon was making slow progress along the trail, having to make several small detours to avoid fallen rock and debris. The horses were tiring, the tonnage taking its toll on their strength.

Reuben Biggs, the driver and Pinkerton agent, guided the wagon to a small, grassy area just off the main trail and drew rein.

'Be dark soon, we best get these horses fed and watered and set up camp for the night,' he said to his partner, Ben Fogg – also of the Pinkerton agency.

Ben, a man of few words but a man you could rely on, heaved his six feet four frame from the hard wooden seat and jumped to the ground. It took a few minutes for both men to ease their backs and legs and get the circulation going again.

The horses were unhitched, tethered, fed and watered then a camp-fire was lit and soon the aroma of a pot of Arbuckles filled the air.

'We got fatback bacon, beans and bread,' Reuben

told his partner.

'Nothin' new there, then,' Ben replied as Reuben brought out the food and a pan.

'Decoy wagon should be in Indian Bar by now,' Reuben said as he placed the pan over the fire and soon the bacon was sizzling.

'Bet they ain't eatin' beans an' bacon!' Ben said as he rolled a quirley and leant back on a smooth rock.

'Well, we'll get our turn, soon as we get to the Feather River.'

'If we get there,' Ben said.

The two men served themselves from the pan and ate in silence.

The noise coming from Latham's Palace was almost deafening, even from where Sheriff Morgan was sitting, still sucking on his pipe.

The night air was cool and a welcome relief from the heat of the daytime.

Still no wagon had appeared and Morgan was now convinced that it had either busted a wheel or, more seriously, had been ambushed. He hoped the former but feared the latter.

Taking out his Hunter, he flipped the lid and checked the time: nine thirty, time for his rounds.

In comparison to the Palace, lights ablaze, a piano, violin, drum and now and then, a banjo as well as the whooping of the crowd inside every time Daisy Rae sang, the rest of Indian Bar seemed like a ghost town.

Sheriff Morgan was tempted to go have a look-see at what was going on in the saloon, but decided against it; he didn't want to know what he was missing.

Turning away from the Palace, he followed his normal routine of checking the doors and windows along the south side of Main Street, before crossing over and doing the same along the north side.

As usual, all was in order. There was not a soul in sight, nor a lamp lit in any of the businesses, so he headed north, down a side street to check on the livery and the few houses that were there.

Oil lamps showed as soft glows through most of the drape-enclosed windows but some of the shacks were in darkness, their occupants either at the Palace or, more likely, asleep.

Morgan turned and continued his rounds, always thorough, even though nothing of any interest ever happened in Indian Bar.

Had he lingered a few minutes longer he would have seen a troop of men arrive at spaced intervals and enter a shack at the far end of the street.

Come first light, Sheriff Brad Morgan had finished his coffee and sucked on his pipe as he filled his saddlebags with coffee, a pot and tin mug and a whole mess of jerky. He'd filled two canteens, which he hung from the pommel, and that completed his needs.

Morgan reckoned if all was well, he'd only be away for the day, if not, well, he'd play it by ear. Leaving a note for his deputy, the sheriff locked up the office, slung his saddle-bag behind the saddle and mounted up.

He walked his horse down a deserted Main Street, taking in the fresh, morning air and the welcome gentle, cool breeze that hit his face. He knew that before too long the sun would be high in the sky and the usual heat build-up would begin.

Despite his fears of what had become of the decoy wagon, Brad Morgan let out a contented sigh. He loved this town, he loved his job and to him, this was the best part of the day.

Reaching the town limits, effectively, the end of his jurisdiction, he kicked his mare into a gentle lope, heading north along the well-worn trail.

The sun, still low in the sky, added a pink hue to the bottom of the few puffy clouds that moved lazily across the clear blue sky, and Morgan began to feel the warmth on his face.

The trail here was level and sandy, but Morgan knew that pretty soon it would start to rise and get rockier as he neared the distant foothills. He knew his mount, fresh, fed and watered, could keep up the easy lope all day if necessary; he also knew that once he began to climb, he'd have to walk the mare. The last thing you wanted out here was a lame horse.

Morgan had been a law officer for nearly thirty years, starting as a lowly deputy, whose job consisted mainly of making coffee and running errands, but he was happy to do these menial tasks as he learned about the law.

The fact that he had survived these past thirty years was evidence of his thoroughness. Approaching fifty, Morgan was as astute and as careful as ever, very little escaped his attention. His attention to detail bordered on fastidiousness, but that never bothered him.

As the trail began to rise, the sand gave way to gravel and shale and small outcrops of flat rock. The sheriff slowed to a walk, his eyes never leaving the trail ahead and the lay of the land either side of the trail.

A lesser man would have missed the sign, but not Brad Morgan. It was common to see buzzards circling high above out here in the wilderness in the early hours of the day, mainly due to the fact that night critters hunted and fought and the escaped wounded often died as the temperature dropped.

But this was different. It seemed that the dozen or so buzzards weren't waiting for their prey to die, but waiting their turn.

Ahead, Brad could hear a faint noise of squabbling birds. He reined in and tilted his head to hear better. No doubt about it, he thought, a whole mess o' birds ahead someplace.

As he got closer, Morgan's senses kicked into action. His eyes were everywhere, searching the ground for anything unusual.

And he found what he was looking for.

The smooth flat rock ahead of him seemed to have small fresh grooves in places and something was missing. It took Brad a moment or two to figure out what it was.

Brad turned in the saddle and stared hard at the trail behind him, where the smooth rocks, worn by wind and rain and man, had a coating of sand over them. When his gaze returned to the trail ahead, there was an area where there was very little sand, as if someone had brushed the trail clear.

Now it could be the wind, he thought, but that was just wishful thinking. Something had happened here. He was convinced.

Dismounting, Brad studied the ground intently before looking up into the clear, blue sky and watched the buzzards lazily circling on a thermal.

The squawking was beginning to fill his brain now and, reluctantly, he led his horse forward, gripping the reins much tighter than was necessary. Twenty, thirty, forty paces, Morgan realized he was counting the steps. Cautiously, he took out his six-gun, keeping his eyes moving from left to right, looking for sign.

He found it.

To his right the smooth rocks were deeply scarred and where the trail petered out, he saw a deep ravine, a cleft between the foothills.

The sound of the birds below was almost deafening now as he approached the lip of the ravine.

Dropping the reins to the ground, he peered down into the darkness.

What he saw was like a scene straight from hell.

An attempt had been made to cover the gory scene below, but the buzzards had cleared most of the tumbleweed and brush to get at the bodies.

The grisly scene was littered with broken limbs and the sound of flesh being ripped off bodies.

Without thinking, Brad fired off two quick shots

into the air.

The squawking rose to a crescendo as the buzzards took flight, the sound of their flapping wings shot past Brad as if he wasn't there. Several buzzards had pieces of flesh clamped into their beaks as they rose, panicked, into the air to join the others circling high above.

Brad reholstered his gun and stared at the macabre scene below him.

As his eyes became more accustomed to the dark shadow, he picked out more and more bodies, their twisted limbs lay in unnatural poses. Then he saw the wagon, shattered, but recognizable.

He took no comfort for thinking he was right in his guess that something bad had happened.

It was far worse than he feared. A massacre.

He stared for long, long minutes at the hell below before looking at the walls of the ravine, searching for a way down. But the walls were almost perpendicular and the ravine some sixty or seventy yards deep, maybe more.

There was no way down. No way to at least make sure there were no survivors. But in his heart, he knew there wouldn't be any.

Now he had two choices: return to town and try and form a posse, or ride on in the hope of coming across the gold wagon and warn them.

He chose the latter, it would take too long to turn back. He had to find that wagon.

# CHAPTER EIGHT

Indian Bar was coming to life.

Shortly after sunrise, traders and merchants were on their way to work. The livery, as always, was the first to open up.

Caleb Green, livery-cum-blacksmith owner, was, like Sheriff Morgan, a creature of habit. Come hell or high water, the animals always came first. He fed and watered them and made sure they hadn't injured themselves during the night.

Satisfied all was well, he then fired up the furnace, raking the embers from the night before and stoking up with a mixture of coal and wood. Next came the coffee. A fifteen minute break to drink coffee and light up the day's first quirley, before mucking out the stalls.

When his daily chores were completed to his satisfaction, Caleb turned his attention to the compound at the rear of the livery, which he had been paid to make secure.

He'd spent the previous two days erecting a higher

fence and making the entrance wider as he was told to expect a wagon any time within the next two days. However, no wagon had arrived and no one had given him any more information as to when he could expect it.

Making sure the compound was still empty, he decided to call on Sheriff Morgan, as the only key to the compound was held by the Pinkerton agents at their insistence.

Reaching the sheriff's office, he found the door still locked and the interior in darkness.

'Hell's teeth!' Caleb muttered. 'Guess the sheriff's overslept.'

Turning on his heels, he almost knocked over the young deputy who had just arrived.

'You goin' in or comin' out?' Clancy Miller asked.

'Cain't be comin' out when the damn office is locked up tight,' Caleb answered in a surly tone.

'Locked?' Clancy replied. 'Sheriff's always here afore me.'

'Well, he ain't here this mornin',' Caleb said.

'Come on in an' I'll get the coffee on, he won't be long,' Clancy said, unlocking the door.

While Clancy stoked up the pot belly stove, Caleb noticed the note on the sheriff's desk addressed to the deputy.

'Hold up there, boy,' Caleb said, picking up the note.

'Mr Green. You can call me Clancy, or you can call me Deputy, but I don't take a likin' to bein' called "boy".'

'No offence, b—, Deputy.' Caleb passed the note over.

Silently, Clancy read the note and then looked up.

'Sheriff's gone out to try and find the wagon,' he said almost to himself.

'What the hell's goin' on?' Caleb demanded.

'Darned if I know,' Clancy answered. 'Sheriff's been tight-lipped ever since them two Pinkerton boys showed up.'

'Well, I cain't hang around here all day. You let me know if'n you hear anything. OK?' Caleb left the office and walked back to his livery.

No sooner had Caleb left than Barker and Swills entered the sheriff's office.

'Mornin', Deputy. Sheriff around?' Barker asked.

'No, sir. The sheriff's out on the trail, looking for the wagon that was supposed to be here yesterday.'

Barker cast a furtive glance at Swills before asking, 'When did he leave?'

'Can't rightly say, but knowin' the sheriff, I'd say first light,' Clancy answered. 'You got a message for him? Or is there anything I can do?'

'No. No, it's OK, Deputy. Nothing important.' Swills touched the brim of his hat and the two men left the office.

Jed Greeley lit up a cigar as he lay in his bunk.

He'd allowed his men to have a drink the night before, two each, no more, but in the cramped and confined space of the small shack, the smell of sweat and alcohol, mixed with tobacco was overpowering.

At least the cigar tasted and smelled good, to him anyway.

One by one his men began to stir and wake up. Yawning, stretching and scratching as they eased their aching limbs up from a night spent on a hard wood floor.

Sunlight filtered through the rags that acted as curtains over the two windows facing the alleyway, shafts of light filled with dust particles as the men stood, grunting to each other, their usual form of communication.

Gun belts were retrieved and strapped on; boots found and, with effort, feet were rammed into them.

Soon, cigarette smoke filled the cabin along with the accompanying coughs of the smokers.

Greeley stood and donned his Stetson, cigar clamped between stained teeth, and walked to one of the windows. He pulled back a dust-laden rag and peered through a hand-made window pane that was more opaque than transparent into the alleyway outside.

Half-sheathed in dark shadow from the rays of the early morning low sun, Greeley could see no movement outside.

He turned and sat down at the rough-wooden table and someone placed a steaming mug of coffee in front of him.

No one had spoken yet, Greeley's men knew better than to speak before Jed spoke. The silence was broken by a sharp rapping at the front door. The lethargy that had seemed to envelope the still asleep men disappeared in an instant. As one, the men drew their six-guns and looked towards Greeley.

Greeley casually relit his cigar and nodded to one of the men. The man stepped forward and opened the door. Standing outside was Amos Barker and Joseph Swills.

Greeley lifted a hand and beckoned the two men in. 'Check the alley,' Greeley growled, and the man nearest the door poked his head out and looked left and right, then closed the door quickly.

'It's empty, boss.'

'You boys go see to the horses, then grab some grub, but not all at once. No more'n two of you together an' don't even acknowledge each other. You got that?' Greeley growled.

'Sure thing, boss,' came the muttered response.

'And no booze!' Greeley added.

One by one, the six men left. Greeley knew that, with Daisy Rae Mahoney in town, there would be plenty of strangers around and his men would just blend in.

The three men sat in silence for a few moments before Swills asked, 'Everything going to plan?'

Greeley sucked on his cigar and let out a thick cloud of blue smoke before answering.

'Yup.'

Swills looked to Amos Barker.

'After last night's performance, the town will be filled tonight as word gets around that Daisy Rae is here,' Barker began. 'But we just learned that the sheriff has gone looking for the dummy wagon.'

'We cleared up pretty good,' Greeley responded.

'Let's hope the sheriff finds nothing, else he might ride on and meet up with the real gold wagon,' Swills said.

'Won't change a thing,' Greeley grunted. 'The gold's as good as ours.'

'Nevertheless, I think we'll ride up the trail a ways, see what we can find.' Swills stood.

'Make sure you get back here before sunset,' was all Greeley said.

Barker and Swills left the shack, leaving Greeley to sit and ponder.

Indian Bar was taken care of, there would be so many people in town that the sheriff and his deputy would find it impossible to cope. So the fact that the sheriff was absent was even better news.

It took Greeley only seconds to decide that the two Pinkerton men had served his needs and were now surplus to his requirements.

He'd see to them on their return.

# CHAPTER NINE

Sheriff Morgan set off at a gallop. Sick to the stomach at what he'd just seen, anger boiled within him.

After ten minutes, he reined in and set the horse to a canter. No need to take it out on my horse, he thought to himself.

He only hoped that he'd meet up with the gold wagon before whoever had committed the atrocity he'd discovered did. His other worry was that the gold wagon might have taken a different route. There was another trail to the north, but it was rarely used these days and Morgan doubted its suitability for a heavily-laden wagon.

Anxiety gnawed at his guts. He didn't think he could face another massacre scene.

But Brad Morgan was made of sterner stuff.

He'd spent the best part of his life as a lawman; being a gopher in his youth he'd made the coffee, brought food from the café, and swept out the endless dust and sand from the sheriff's office. All without complaint and his efforts were duly noted as, on his eighteenth birthday, he was made a deputy.

Even as he rode, Brad Morgan couldn't help but smile to himself as these thoughts unexpectedly drifted through his mind. Subconsciously, maybe he thought this was his last job as sheriff. He had a bad feeling about this.

Too much change in too short a time always put Morgan on edge. Even at the height of the gold rush, he kept law and order in Indian Bar with a rod of iron.

Admittedly, drink was the major cause of any trouble, but he always managed to calm the drunks down, lock them up for the night and, after a statutory fine, release them the next day only for them to get drunk again.

It seemed a never-ending cycle.

Never-ending, that was, until the seam ran dry and the itinerant gold-panners drifted off to pastures new in their endless search for the mother-lode.

Few made it.

He'd been riding for over an hour. The heat from the early morning sun was beginning to build up as its rays cut through a clear blue sky and Morgan knew that in the next couple of hours, he'd be sweating and uncomfortable in the saddle. But still he pressed on at a gentle canter.

The trail was rising all the time and becoming

more treacherous as the soft sand disappeared altogether and stone and rock took over.

His mount was sure-footed, but still, the sheriff kept a close eye on the trail ahead. To his right, he could hear the gurgling sounds of water as the trail neared the Feather River as it made its way down from the still distant mountain range.

Although he hadn't ridden this trail for many years, he remembered a point where trail and river came close. Close enough to fill his canteens and let his horse take a rest and drink the cool, fresh mountain water.

Another hour passed and, true to his memory, he saw the river. His mount snorted and whinnied as it, too, smelled the tang of water vapour in the air.

'Easy, boy,' the sheriff said, gently rubbing his horse's neck. 'We're nearly there.'

Ten minutes later, the sheriff reined in on a small, sandy beach. It hadn't changed a bit. He'd heard of, but never actually seen, beaches out West down Los Angeles way. He'd been told stories of miles of golden sand that ran down to the Pacific Ocean. Water so vast you couldn't see the end of it.

Morgan had taken these tales with a pinch of salt until a carpet-bagger had passed through town selling what he called 'photee-graffs' and one in particular had caught Brad's attention: a picture of a long sandy beach in front of a huge expanse of ocean. He'd bought the picture and it adorned his office wall. He swore that one day he'd travel out further West and see this beach for himself.

But for now, he contented himself with this tiny stretch of sand. He dismounted and his horse needed no encouragement to walk forward and start drinking.

Brad stretched his aching frame. It had been a while since he'd been a-saddle for this length of time and his rump let him know it.

He knelt on one knee and took out his pipe. Adding fresh tobacco, he tamped it down and lit it, puffing thick smoke into the air as it caught.

He stared at the fast flowing river, hypnotized by the constant movement. Why can't the world be like this place, he thought. Peaceful. Serene, that's the word he was looking for. Serene!

He sat for a few more minutes before he stood up, grabbed his canteens and emptied the already tepid water and filled them with the cool water of the river. He then took off his Stetson, cupped his hands and splashed water on his face several times.

On another day, he would have stripped to his long johns and sat in the water until he'd frozen his butt off. But not today.

Today he had to get a move on.

Reaching into his war bag, he grabbed a handful of oats, put them in his hat and fed his horse. He shook the oat dust from his hat, wiped the inside with his bandanna, then his forehead, before re-mounting.

It seemed every muscle in his body was crying out. The short rest had stiffened him up a little and it took a while to get some semblance of comfort on

67

the hard, Western saddle.

The trail rose swiftly now, away from the river, and Morgan could chance no more than a gentle trot; if his horse went lame out here, his own chances of survival were minimal.

Reuben Biggs and Ben Fogg were unaware of the situation as they broke camp and harnessed the horses. They'd taken it in turns to mount guard during the night, two hours on, two hours off. Even with a broken sleep pattern, they both felt refreshed after breakfast and coffee – lots of coffee. But now it was time to press on. They had to reach their destination, just south of Indian Bar, where it was deemed safe to launch the wagon as the waters were a gentle, slow, south-west current.

As long as they bypassed the town itself – unseen – they were sure they'd make it.

What neither man was looking forward to, was launching the Conestoga.

No amount of assurance or practice had filled the two men with much confidence. It was a risky business and basically Reuben and Ben were doing it for the large bonus promised on completion of their task.

Childhood friends, they had joined the agency together and their ultimate aim was to save enough money to get themselves a small horse ranch, preferably near an army base, where horses were in great demand.

Climbing aboard the wagon, Reuben took the

reins while Ben checked his Winchester and both his handguns, Colts, each loaded with six instead of the safer, five bullets.

'Ready?' Reuben said.

Ben cocked the Winchester and laid it across his lap before answering, 'As I'll ever be.'

Reuben flicked the reins, and yelled, 'Giddup!'

'You really think "giddup" makes any sense to them animals?' Ben asked.

'Hell, no. But you gotta shout something!'

'Why?'

'I dunno. Just seems the right thing, is all,' Reuben answered, and winked.

'You're plumb loco,' Ben said, smiling.

'Don't ya jus' know it.' Reuben laughed.

The trail, now on a gentle slope, was littered with loose stones, washed down by wind and rain over the years and made the going a rough ride.

Speech was almost impossible with sudden jolts shaking the men to their bones.

'Ya better slow it down a tad,' Ben yelled. 'We don't want a busted wheel or axle.'

'Woah, there,' Reuben shouted as he pulled back on the reins and put his foot on the brake, slowing the wagon down to walking pace. 'Better?' he grinned at Ben.

'I'll tell you once my teeth stop rattling around,' said Ben.

'Maybe it'd be a good idea if one of us scouted ahead, in case there's any rocks that need shifting,' Reuben said.

'I'll do that with pleasure,' Ben said, relieved to get off the wagon for a spell.

Ben jumped from the hard wooden seat and stretched his back before walking a few paces in front of the lead pair.

He idly kicked at a few stones and small rocks as he walked. Ahead there was a sharp left-hand bend in the trail so Ben put a hand up to stop the wagon while he disappeared to check the way ahead. The last thing either man wanted was an unwelcome surprise.

Rounding the bend, Ben could see the trail as it meandered down the slopes of the foothills for at least half a mile. He stopped to take in the view; wiping his neck and forehead with his bandanna, he marvelled at the wonders of Nature. Taking a deep breath of the now warm clean air, he was about to return to give the all clear when he saw, in the distance, a lone rider.

He stepped to the side of the trail, just in case he could be seen, and took out his army issue telescope.

He sighted on the rider, but the distance was too great to make out any great detail, except that the man was not in any sort of hurry, obviously taking care of his mount. Ben then trained the telescope behind the rider, in case he was a forward scout for a gang, maybe. He could see no further movement, but he waited a few minutes to make sure. He put the telescope away and ran back to the wagon.

'Rider approaching,' he called out to Reuben.

'Just the one?' Reuben asked.

'Far as I could tell, unless there's more travelling

way back behind him. I could just see the one,' Ben stated.

'OK. We'll hold up here and wait.' Reuben locked the brake and reached for his rifle as he left the driver's seat and leapt to the ground.

'Ain't no rush, Reuben, he's at least a mile away,' Ben said. 'I'll stay at the bend in the trail, you take cover on the right of the trial, there's a boulder there to hide behind.'

'Yes, boss.' Reuben grinned.

'OK, OK.' Ben took out a cheroot and lit it. 'I reckon we got ten to fifteen minutes before he reaches us, so got plenty of time to get ready.'

Sheriff Morgan carefully picked his way up the rocky slope, his eyes glued to the trail ahead as it rose towards the foothills.

The temperature was steadily rising, heat already rising from the smooth rocks and shimmering ahead of him.

He reined in and, removing his Stetson, wiped his brow, then took a mouthful of water. Although he had two full canteens, he had no idea where, or even if, the gold wagon was nearby. He could be out here for days with no guarantee of finding a waterhole.

Digging his heels in to the horse's flanks, he rode on, climbing ever higher. His one consolation was, if he reached the mountains, the air would be cooler.

But that was a big if. Doubts still filled his mind. What he couldn't fathom was why the decoy wagon had been attacked. Did whoever was responsible know it was a decoy? Or did they think it was the real thing?

Moreover, how did they know about the shipment in the first place?

So many questions, and no answers to any of them.

Clancy Miller was out of his depth.

Indian Bar was filling up with more people than he'd ever seen in his young life.

Miners, trappers, panners and general riff-raff had started to arrive in town as news that Daisy Rae was performing again spread like wildfire.

It was only ten in the morning and already several brawls and gunfire had been heard at the north end of town.

The town council seemed impotent. Clancy had tried to see the mayor and get some help but had just been told to wait for the sheriff's return. He'd know what to do.

Clancy's protests were ignored as the majority of the town's council were storeowners and two saloon owners. All they saw were dollar signs.

It was exactly the scenario Jed Greeley had hoped for.

Chaos.

His men had returned to the shack after watering and feeding their horses and grabbing a bite to eat in the overcrowded café, where their presence had been totally ignored.

'Town sure is packed, boss,' one of his men remarked.

'That was the idea,' Greeley grated.

'What's the plan now, boss?' another man asked.

'We got ourselves some driftwood to cut free,' Greeley said.

The gang looked puzzled.

'The gold wagon is due to bypass Indian Bar sometime this afternoon.' Greeley paused to let this information sink in. 'Before that, I want Barker and Swills taken care of. *Comprende?*'

'Sure thing, boss. No problem.' A man stood and checked his Colt Peacemaker.

'Hold your horses,' Greeley said. 'I want you to stake out that boarding house they're stayin' in. I figure they eat there as well, but when they leave, follow them. The town's packed out, you shouldn't have any trouble bein' spotted.'

'Then what?' Greeley was asked.

'I want no shootin'. Use your knives an' make it look like a robbery. Take 'em down in some alley an' come straight back here. Understand?'

'Consider it done, boss. '

The men stood as one and left the shack as Greeley poured himself a third cup of coffee.

'Cole,' Greeley called after one of the men. 'I want you to head east up the trail and see what you can find. Keep your eyes peeled and watch for any sign. You remember where we hit that wagon?'

'Sure do, boss.'

'Well, see if everything's as we left it, then git back here to me. Savvy?'

'On my way, boss,' the man said, and headed for his horse.

Amos Barker and Joseph Swills enjoyed their home-cooked breakfast at Ma Biggs's boarding house.

'More coffee, boys?' Ma Biggs asked.

'No, thank you, ma'am. Don't think I could manage anything else for a week,' Amos replied.

'That was a mighty fine breakfast, ma'am. Jus' like my ma used to make,' Joseph added.

'Well, thank you, boys. I like to see my men folk well fed.' Ma Biggs gave a broad smile and went back to her kitchen.

'We better go check with Greeley, make sure there's no problem,' Amos said.

'I could do with a walk,' Joseph said. 'My belly's fit to burstin'.'

The two men stood as Ma Biggs came into the small parlour.

'Dinner's at six,' she said. 'Stew and dumplings, an' I'll make apple pie and get some cream in.' She beamed at both men.

'We might not be back by then, Mrs Biggs. We got business – official business – to do today,' Amos said, with a mock sad expression on his face.

'Well, I'll keep some back for you, easy to keep it warm.' She smiled and went back to her kitchen.

Both men left the boarding house and stepped out onto the bustling street.

'Seems word got round all right,' Amos said.

'Sure did. I bet this town ain't had so many people in it – ever!' Joseph grinned.

'We're gonna be rich men, Joe, rich men.'

Both men failed to see the Greeley gang standing on the boardwalk opposite the boarding house. They split into two groups of three. Three men followed the Pinkerton men, the other three ducked down a side alley.

Swills and Barker, oblivious to the danger they were in, walked down the street until they reached the small side street where the Greeley gang were holed up.

Turning right into the narrow street, they saw three men approaching. Amos recognized them straight away, but wasn't concerned: after all, they were all in the same gang. Joseph, however, was more leery. He stopped in his tracks. Neither man saw the other three men approach them from behind.

Too late, Joseph felt their presence. He turned, attempting to draw his gun, but he didn't get the chance. The eight-inch blade cut short his life as it pierced his left side in an upwards thrust before it entered his heart.

He dropped to the ground like a stone.

Dead.

Amos, too, was a fraction too late. He turned as he drew his weapon, but his throat was slit from behind, he collapsed and lay writhing as a pool of blood spread around him. Within two minutes he was dead.

The gang members began to rifle through their pockets, taking anything of value, including both men's guns and Amos's pocket watch, given to him by his father.

Five minutes later, the street was deserted. Only the two dead men remained.

# CHAPTER TEN

Sheriff Morgan was making steady progress up the gradient, making every effort to spare his horse. Three quarters of the way up, he dismounted and poured some water into his hat and let the animal drink.

He took out his pipe and pushed a pinch of tobacco in it and lit up, enjoying the taste as the smoke filled his lungs.

Morgan took a few moments to gaze at the scenery. To his right, a sheer rock face, the beginning of the Sierra Nevada mountain range. To his left, a heavily wooded landscape that gave way to a flat, fertile plain that followed the north edge of the Feather River.

The cloudless sky, lit by the blazing fury of the sun, seemed endless. In the far distance he could still see buzzards circling high above; doubtless, he thought, it would be a few days yet before their grizzly work would be finished.

He looked ahead, following the trail as it climbed,

before it disappeared around a bend and knew from previous visits, that the trail meandered upwards for maybe a few hundred yards, before slowly beginning to descend once more eastwards, heading towards Utah Territory.

He stuffed his pipe back into his vest pocket and remounted and urged the horse onwards. 'Easy, boy, hopefully not far to go now,' he said out loud.

The horse whinnied as if in reply.

Ten minutes later, he reached the bend.

'Hold it right there, fella,' a voice boomed out.

'And keep your hands where we can see 'em,' came another voice.

Morgan did exactly as he was told. Both hands in the air, he yelled, 'I'm jus' gonna lift my vest with my left hand and show you something,' he said, in a voice with more confidence than he felt.

'Slow an' easy,' came the reply.

Morgan lifted one side of his leather vest, revealing his sheriff's badge.

Assessing the situation quickly, Morgan noted the wagon and six parked further up the trail and, from the sound of the two voices, one man on each side of the trail.

'I'm looking for the Pinkerton men, to warn them,' Morgan shouted out.

'Throw down your sidearm and unsheathe that rifle, two fingers only, we got you covered,' he was ordered.

Slowly and carefully, Morgan lowered his right arm and, using thumb and forefinger, pulled out his Colt by the butt and let it drop to the ground, making sure it hit a patch of sand. Then, reaching behind him, he pulled out the rifle and dropped that too.

'OK, now get down nice an' easy.'

Easing his aching limbs over the saddle, Morgan dropped to the ground.

'Keep those hands high,' bellowed a voice.

Reuben and Ben then revealed themselves, both keeping their Winchesters trained on Morgan.

'State your name and business,' Reuben ordered.

'I'm Sheriff Brad Morgan of Indian Bar, I came out here to warn you fellas that I suspect a heist. I already discovered the dummy wagon. Everyone is dead.'

Morgan paused to let this information sink in.

'How'd you find out about this shipment?' Ben asked.

Morgan went on to explain, telling the men about the two Pinkerton agents.

'Can't say I know all the agents,' Reuben said, 'but I sure as hell ain't heard of a Barker and Swills. You, Ben?'

'Nope, new to me,' Ben replied.

'Well, they mentioned the Greeley gang,' the sheriff added.

'Hot dog!' Ben exclaimed. 'We bin after that gang for a long time.'

'What the hell do we do now?' Reuben said sombrely.

'Well, we can't go back,' Ben said.

'Indian Bar is jam-packed, I can't even be sure the Greeley gang aren't there already,' Morgan said. 'You two boys mind if'n I put my arms down now?'

Ben looked at Reuben before replying. 'Sure, go ahead, Sheriff.'

'Thanks, ain't used to this much ridin' and sure ain't used to this much excitement.'

'Any suggestions, Sheriff, as to what to do next?' asked Reuben. 'I guess you know the terrain better'n we do.'

'Well, I know you were meant to follow the trail to the north of Indian Bar, but I reckon that's too dangerous now. The only thing I can suggest is getting into the Feather River to the east of the town and, if that darn thing floats, use the river to the south of town. It's a mighty long stretch 'til you reach the Sacramento River. You sure that thing will float?' Morgan said as he removed his Stetson and scratched his head.

'Hell, we only know what we've been told,' Reuben said. 'We seen it float all right, but that was in a small lake with no current. Engineers said it would float and we could steer it with a tiller that's fitted at the rear of the wagon. Trouble is, we ain't had much practice.'

'Mind if'n I pick my guns up now?' Morgan asked.

'Sure,' Ben said. But the sheriff noticed that Reuben had raised his rifle again.

Bending down, Morgan first picked up the Winchester and placed that in his saddle boot. Then, using thumb and forefinger, picked up the Colt, blew some sand off it and replaced it in his holster.

He walked forward with an outstretched hand

towards Ben. 'Call me Brad,' he said, and the two men shook hands.

'I'm Ben and this here is Reuben.' Ben reached inside his trail coat and brought out a card, showing he was a Pinkerton agent. Reuben did the same and held out his hand to the sheriff.

'So,' Morgan said, 'how in tarnation does this thing work?'

The three men walked towards the converted Conestoga.

It was Ben who began the explanation.

'Well, we seen this done a few times. We back the wagon into the water, then unhitch the horses. One of us stays on the wagon and use that there pole to keep the wagon in position.

'Then, with two of us aboard, we pull out these here pins that keep the wheels on. After that, we both use the poles to push the wagon out deeper into the river and, when we start to float, we kick the wheels off.'

'Sounds like a stupid idea to me,' Morgan said.

'Well, if'n it don't work, we'll be stuck on the side of the river, cos once those pins come out it'll be nigh on impossible to put them back in.' Ben smiled. 'All that gold just waitin' to be picked off.'

'We'll soon find out,' Morgan stated. ''Bout a mile an' a half yonder, the trail gets dang close to the river. Current ain't too strong there, but there's sand an' I got no idea how deep it is there. But that's the only place to get close enough to the river to launch this contraption. As I said, I figure if'n you try heading through the north trail, you'll run into trouble.'

'Well, seems we have no choice then,' Reuben said.

The door to the sheriff's office burst open and Abe Mortimer shouted, 'You better get out here, Sheriff!'

Clancy looked up. He was seated at the sheriff's desk with his head in his hands.

'Sheriff ain't here, Abe,' Clancy said.

'Well, where in the hell is he? There's two dead fellas lying in the street, stabbed by the looks of it.'

'So go get the undertaker,' Clancy said. 'Ain't nothing I can do. Town's full of strangers.'

'It's them two Pinkerton fellas,' Abe told him.

'What?' Clancy got reluctantly to his feet.

'You heard right, them Pinkerton boys,' Abe reiterated.

Clancy reached for his hat and grabbed one of the Winchesters from the gun rack and, as an afterthought, picked up a box of .45 slugs.

'What in hell you need that fer?' Abe asked.

'You never know, 'sides, the sheriff never goes on a case without a rifle. Never know what you come up against,' Clancy said.

The two men left the office and made their way to the scene of the killings.

A group of townsfolk and strangers formed a ring around the gruesome sight of the two men. A pool of blood almost surrounded the bodies and already flies had descended on the grisly scene.

'Jeez!' Clancy almost gagged as he fought his way

through the mêlée. He ignored the few sniggers that went up around him and fought the bile he felt rising in his throat.

'Any of you men see anything?' he asked in a voice that he wanted to sound firm and commanding, but instead came out a mite shaky.

His question was answered with a series of grunts and shaking heads.

'Abe, go fetch the undertaker, I'll see what identification they have,' Clancy said. 'The rest of you men can clear off now, there ain't nothing to see here.'

The crowd began to drift off grudgingly, leaving only Clancy and a couple of stragglers in the alleyway.

Clancy got down on one knee, careful to avoid the blood and flies. In the hot sun, the blood had turned from bright red to a dull crimson and in some places black. Gingerly, he went through both men's pockets.

He found nothing.

Abe returned with the undertaker, Luther McGovern, a second generation Scot with a scrawny body and taciturn manner that didn't make him the most popular of residents in Indian Bar.

His weasely-black eyes took in the scene with no more emotion than had he been looking at a blank wall.

'They got any money?' Luther asked, spitting into the ground.

'None that I can find,' Clancy said.

'Then who's gonna pay? I ain't in this fer my health, ya know!'

'Guess the town will,' Clancy replied. 'Maybe get the money back from the Pinkerton Agency later.'

'Hmmm. OK. But you heard what he said, Abe,' Luther said.

'Yeah, I heard. Go get your fancy hearse, Luther,' Abe said.

Luther stomped off, then, turning, 'I better get paid fer this!' he growled and disappeared around the corner of the alley.

'They got nothin' on 'em, Clancy?' Abe asked.

'Clean as a whistle. Even their side irons are gone.'

'Well, with all these here strangers in town, I guess it had to happen sooner or later.' Abe sighed.

'What?' Clancy asked.

'Robbery, o' course. What else?' Abe reasoned.

'You reckon that's all it is?' Clancy stood and looked away from the bodies.

'Sure, what else?'

Cole Cairney had ridden as if the very Devil was after him.

He'd reached the site of the massacre of the dummy wagon and inspected the area thoroughly, and now he had to tell Greeley what he'd found.

He steered his foam-flecked mount into the alley just as Clancy and Abe were helping the undertaker wrap and load the two bodies into a covered flatbed.

Cole didn't notice in his haste to get to Greeley, but the three men stood and watched as Cole jumped from his horse and hammered on the door of the last shack on the right.

'Hmm,' Abe said as he stood upright.

'What?' Clancy asked.

'Fella seemed mighty anxious, there,' Abe replied. 'Didn't know the old Stoner place had been sold.'

'Well, you don't know everything,' Luther grumbled. 'Let's git this last one loaded, time is—'

'Money, yeah I know,' Abe said. 'There ain't much goes on I don't know about,' he added, rubbing his stubbled chin.

They loaded the second body and without preamble, Luther climbed aboard the wagon and drove off, shouting over his shoulder, 'I'll bury 'em tomorrow.' And with that, he was gone.

'Maybe I'll check that shack out,' Clancy said.

'I'd go to the bank first,' Abe advised. 'No sense in creating waves unnecessarily.'

'Yeah, good point, Abe,' Clancy said as he checked the ground where the two men were killed. 'Nothing to look at here. Too many busybodies trampled all over the place.'

Greeley rose slowly and drew his sidearm as he walked towards the door.

'Who's there?' he said.

'It's me, Cole,' came the reply.

Greeley opened the door and made sure it was Cole before letting him in.

'Someone's done found 'em, boss,' Cole blurted out.

'How can you be sure?' Greeley asked.

'Prints. One man, one horse.'

'Coulda been anyone,' Greeley said.

'Coulda bin, but they didn't turn back. Night breeze clears most track, these were fresh. No more'n three, maybe four hours by my reckoning.' Cole wiped his forehead.

A knock on the door interrupted the two men.

Again, Greeley drew his gun. 'Who is it?'

'Us, boss, we took care o' business.'

'Open the door, Cole,' Greeley ordered.

'Took a walk around town, boss,' one of the men stated. 'Found out the sheriff rode out at first light.'

'Did he now?' Greeley sat and pondered this information.

Greeley sat quietly, his men stood and waited. The longer they waited, the more they exchanged glances and fidgeted.

After five long minutes, Greeley stood.

'Get your gear together. Change of plan. We're heading north to pick up the trail there. If'n that wagon's running to time, we'll run slap into 'em. Now move!'

# CHAPTER ELEVEN

With Sheriff Morgan leading the way, the wagon made steady progress down the slope. Reuben's foot was beginning to ache as he kept pressure on the brake to stop the wagon going too fast. Smoke was rising from the front right wheel as friction took its toll.

The team of six horses were fighting to keep their hoofs steady on the sometimes sandy, sometimes rocky trail. The weight of the wagon behind them was straining every muscle in their sturdy bodies.

Thirty minutes later, they reached the bottom of the slope and Reuben reined in to give both himself and the horse team a rest.

Morgan dismounted and took his canteen from the pommel as both Reuben and Ben dropped to the ground, easing their aching bodies from the uncomfortable ride down the slope.

'How far 'til we near the river?' Ben asked.

'No more'n a mile, I figure,' the sheriff replied.

'It's fairly flat from here on in, but the trail gets a might sandier.'

'How close is that to the fork where we were supposed to take the north trail?' asked Reuben.

'That's around two, maybe three miles further on an' there's a bit of a rise before you reach the fork,' Brad said.

'We best keep moving,' Ben said. 'If the Greeley gang are gonna make a move it'll be sooner rather than later.'

'How the hell did he find out in the first place?' Reuben wondered out loud.

'Beats me, but if he knew there was a dummy wagon, he'll also know your route and roughly what time to expect you,' Morgan said.

'Musta bin an inside job,' Ben said.

'Had to be,' Reuben agreed.

'Right.' Reuben climbed aboard the wagon. 'Let's get goin'.'

---

Clancy took Abe's advice and wandered down to the bank. If anyone knew anything about the old Stoner place, Mr Morrison, the bank manager would.

'Howdy, Deputy,' Hank, as ever on duty, greeted Clancy. He was a tad long in the tooth to be a bank guard, but then, nothing ever happened in Indian Bar anyway.

'Mr Morrison in?' Clancy asked.

'Sure is, ain't he always.' Hank laughed and then coughed at the effort.

Clancy walked up to the side door at the counter

and knocked.

A peep hole opened up, revealing the pinched features of James Jones, the young head teller.

'Yes?'

'I wanna see Mr Morrison,' Clancy said.

'Do you have an appointment?' Jones asked.

Already, Clancy's hackles began to rise.

'No, I don't have any appointment, I'm here on official business,' Clancy said through gritted teeth.

'And what might that be?' Jones asked.

'That's for me and Mr Morrison to discuss,' Clancy said. 'Now go and tell him I'm waiting.'

The peep hole closed and Clancy took off his hat and mopped his forehead, and waited.

And waited.

After waiting for nearly ten minutes, Clancy began to lose patience. Taking out his revolver, he used the butt to bang on the door. So loud was the banging that the bank's activity came to a standstill and a silence descended as everyone looked at Clancy.

The peep hole opened again and the pinched face of an indignant Jones appeared once more.

Clancy cocked the Colt and thrust the barrel on Jones's forehead.

'Open this damn door now or I'm arresting you for impeding the course of justice!'

Clancy wasn't absolutely sure of his ground here, but he hoped the bluff would work.

There was, what seemed in the silence of the bank, a deafening clunk as the bolt was drawn back and the door creaked open inwards.

'That's more like it,' Clancy said as he re-holstered his sidearm and stepped through to the inner sanctum of the bank.

A white sign with black lettering was pinned to a highly polished wooden door: Bank Manager: Mr James Morrison. Clancy knocked once and entered.

A startled Morrison immediately stood and glared at the young deputy.

'What is the meaning of this, Deputy?' he bellowed.

'I'm sure sorry to disturb you, Mr Morrison, but there's been a double murder near the old Stoner place. Them Pinkerton men have been killed an' I saw a stranger enter Stoner's shack. I wonder if you could tell me if'n the place has been sold or rented out recently?' Clancy burst the words out in one breath.

'Good Lord,' Morrison said and sat down again behind his huge desk. 'This is terrible news, especially in the light of—' He stopped short, not knowing whether the young deputy had any knowledge of the gold shipment. 'Where's the sheriff?' he asked in a calmer voice.

'Rode out at sunrise. The wagon never arrived,' Clancy said. 'Now, about the Stoner place?'

'Yes, yes, of course.' Morrison went to a filing cabinet and pulled out a sheaf of papers. He flicked through them and looked up at Clancy.

'Why, it was rented out to the Pinkerton men. Mr Amos Barker and Mr Joseph Swills. They rented it for one week only. Paid in cash.' Morrison closed the file and returned it to the cabinet.

'Thank you, sir. That's mighty interestin' to know.' Clancy touched the brim of his hat and turned to go. Halfway through the door he said, in a loud voice, 'You might inform your teller here, Jones, to show a bit more respect to the law in future, I darn near arrested him for leaving me hanging around waitin' to see you.'

Clancy smiled as he closed the door, knowing that everyone in the bank had heard his comment.

Several pairs of eyes followed Clancy as he headed for the exit. Hank stepped forward and winked at him as he passed and in a low voice said, 'Glad someone took that young upstart down a peg or two,' and smiling, he opened the door for Clancy.

Greeley led his men out of Indian Bar, heading north to pick up the trail that led south almost to Rich Bar, a small settlement that, like Indian Bar, had seen better days. The town lay between a tributary of the Sacramento River and the Feather River and, just south-east, was where the wagon was due to be launched into the river for its journey to Sacramento.

The seven men rode in silence at a steady canter, with Greeley leading the way. He'd already surveyed the territory as soon as he'd found out about the shipment; it was easy to persuade poorly paid agents with the sight of golden eagles and a promise of a share of the takings.

It was over an hour's hard ride to reach their destination, but Greeley had no doubt they'd reach the river well before the wagon.

If the wagon made it that far.


Clancy was at his wits' end. He didn't have the experience to deal with this mess. He knew that the fact that the Pinkerton men had hired the old Stoner place had some relevance. But who the hell was in there? And was it a coincidence that Swills and Barker had been murdered less than a hundred feet from the shack?

Without the sheriff, he didn't know what to do.

He made his way along Main Street and, although he didn't know it, he was heading straight for the alley the men had been killed in and the Stoner place.

He turned left into the alley and stopped. Surprised at finding where he was.

Then he made up his mind. He'd better go see exactly who was in the shack.

He adjusted his gun belt, straightened his bandanna and walked to the shack. Hesitating only briefly as he made sure his deputy's badge was visible, he knocked three times on the dilapidated wooden door of the old shack.

There was no response, so he knocked again, calling out, 'Hello, the house.'

There was a simple bar latch on the door and Clancy lifted it and the door swung open on rusty hinges.

Inside it was dark. There was only one window and that was covered with a dirty sack, letting very little light in.

Clancy called 'hello' again, but it was obvious that the one room shack was empty.

Taking no chances, Clancy drew his pistol and stepped inside.

The smells were almost unbearable: sweat and stale cigar smoke. A cigar stub was in a tin mug set on the table and was still smoking. Whoever had been in here had only just left. He noted the makeshift cots that had been left behind, six plus a proper bed in one corner.

But why would they leave now? Did they know the Pinkerton men, or did they kill them because they were freeloading in the shack?

Seemed unlikely. But then again, he thought, the Pinkerton men were staying at Ma Biggs's boarding house.

So why rent a shack?

There was no food visible, and the stove was almost out. Clearly, there was nothing here to give a clue as to who had been staying there. Except there were seven places for sleeping.

Seven men!

Closing the door behind him, Clancy decided to see Abe and tell him what he'd found out. It was pointless involving the mayor or the town council, the sheriff had always told him they were useless in any situation.

Abe Mortimer was working on a hair-trigger when Clancy entered the gunsmith's shop. He had a workshop out back and a small shooting range beyond that, but he liked working in the shop, behind the glass-topped counter containing various makes of weapons.

He sat on a high stool, a small vice fixed to the counter containing the firing mechanism of a Colt Peacemaker and Abe, eyeglasses perched on the end of his nose, was slowly and deliberately using a file.

Abe never rushed.

'How's it goin', young fella?' Abe asked without looking up.

'I saw Mr Morrison,' Clancy said.

'And?'

'The shack was rented by the two dead men,' Clancy told him.

Abe blew iron filings off the mechanism, placed the file on the counter and removed his eyeglasses.

Clancy went on to tell him that the shack was empty but there were signs that at least seven people had been staying there.

Abe was thoughtful as he digested this news. Then, 'Now that don't make no sense. Brad told me them two Pinkerton men has told him and the bank manager that the Greeley gang were planning a heist of some sort, he didn't say what or where, but there was s'posed to be a wagon comin' through late yesterday.'

'There's somethin' darn fishy going on here and I jus' cain't get my head around it,' Clancy said.

'Come on, Deputy, I'll close up fer a while. Let's go check out that shack again,' Abe said.

'OK, but I can't see what—'

'You check round the back?' Abe asked.

'Well, no.'

'If'n there were seven men in there, they'd need seven horses and they'd sure leave a sign,' Abe said.

'Damn!' Clancy said. 'I shoulda thought of that!'

'Don't matter none,' Abe said. 'As long as one of us did, eh?' He smiled.

'I got a lot to learn, Abe,' Clancy said.

'You'll do fine, young'un. Come on, let's go.'

Abe was right. To the rear of the shack was a hitch rail and enough horse shit to fertilize a corn field.

'Plenty of sign here, Deputy,' Abe said. 'Maybe we oughta do us some tracking.'

'I need to get a posse,' Clancy said. 'If'n them fellas had something to do with the killin's, then we got just cause.'

'True,' Abe said, 'but you really think you're gonna get a posse when tonight's the last night Daisy Rae's is in town?'

'Damn!' Clancy said again. 'I wanted to see her again, too.'

'Well, Deputy, seems to me you got a choice to make. The sheriff ain't here so that makes you the only representative of the law in town. Now, you can ignore this situation and face the consequences when the sheriff gets back, or accept the responsibility that your job entails. What's it to be?'

'I know what I gotta do,' Clancy said. 'First off I'm gonna see the mayor. I can't leave town with no law enforcement an' I reckon it's down to him to get some deputies sworn in. Don't you think?'

'Can't argue with that,' Abe said. 'I'll come with you.'

'To see the mayor?'

'I mean I'll ride with you. I figure we head on up the trail and see if'n we can find the sheriff. What do you think?'

'OK. Meet me at the livery in one hour,' Clancy said. 'That'll give me time to find the mayor and grab some provisions.'

'I'll sort out weapons and ammunition.'

The two men parted and, despite his feelings of inadequacy, Clancy was encouraged by Abe's faith in him and he felt determined to find the killers of the two Pinkerton agents.

Abe, despite his age, was tingling like a young kid again. He hadn't had this much excitement, well, ever, he thought.

He busied himself gathering together four brand new Colt .45s and two of the latest Winchesters, also .45 calibre, and a dozen boxes of slugs. Enough, he thought, to tackle an army.

Donning a new leather gun belt, he loved the smell and the feel of the hand-tooled leather. And the way it creaked as he fastened the buckle.

It felt right. He felt like a man again.

Opening one of the ammo boxes, he inserted five bullets into each of the handguns, making sure the empty chamber was aligned with the firing pin. He didn't want any accidents.

He put one of the Colts into his holster, he hadn't worn a gun for many years and the weight of the weapon on his skinny hips felt good and reassuring.

Next he loaded twelve slugs each into the two

96

Winchesters and placed them, the three Colts and ammunition into his war bag.

He was ready.

Now he had forty minutes to wait.

He made a cup of coffee, lit a cigarette and puffed contentedly.

Waiting.

Clancy was far from content. It took him twenty minutes to track down the mayor who, flustered as ever, was trying to persuade Clancy to wait for the sheriff and not do anything rash. The mayor didn't want the responsibility and panic was building in his short, fat frame.

But Clancy left him no choice. The town was packed with men from all over the territory set on seeing Daisy Rae Mahoney perform and the town needed some sort of law enforcement.

Eventually, the mayor agreed to see what he could do in recruiting volunteers to act as deputies until Sheriff Morgan returned.

Satisfied, but nevertheless not trusting the mayor totally, Clancy went to the general store and put in an official requisition for provisions to last three days. He had no idea how long it would take, so the three days was a pure guess.

Gus McDonald, the storekeeper, made sure Clancy signed for everything. Although a member of the town council, he knew how slow the town was in paying its debts.

Clancy left the store, clutching a bag filled with coffee, beans, fat bacon, jerky and fresh biscuits.

97

Returning to the sheriff's office, he helped himself to a coffee pot, two tin mugs and a skillet.

'That should do it,' he said aloud. Then decided to leave a note for the sheriff – just in case.

Taking a deep breath, he locked the office and made his way to the livery stables.

# CHAPTER TWELVE

The progress of the gold wagon was slow. Much slower than anticipated.

The trail, having left the foothills, was sandier and the weight of the wagon was testing the team of six horses as well as the driver.

On several occasions, one of the wagon's wheels would sink into the soft sand and get bogged down. This then necessitated the three men digging out the sand to form a ramp and inserting sacking under the wheel to get it free.

Since the demise of the gold rush locally, the trail was little used so the sand was not compacted by constant use.

The horses were tiring quickly and both Reuben and Ben knew they had to reach the river as soon as possible so the animals could rest and drink, but their painfully slow progress was beginning to worry all three men.

Then catastrophe struck. One of the animals pulled up lame and the wagon ground to a halt.

'Just what we needed,' Reuben remarked as he jumped to the ground to inspect the animal's hind leg. 'Looks busted, hoof got stuck in a gopher hole by the looks of it.'

'Damn,' Ben said. 'Been slow enough with a full team, you reckon five can manage?'

'We got far to go, Sheriff?' Reuben asked.

'Well, by my reckoning it's a mile at least,' Brad answered.

'Ben, unhitch the poor animal, I'll have to put him down,' Reuben said.

Ben nodded and silently unhitched the rear right animal. The horse seemed to know its fate. The whites of its eyes showed and it tried to rear up, but the useless leg wouldn't allow it.

Reuben led the limping animal back down the trail and then veered to the left. Taking out his Colt, he cocked the hammer and muttered quietly, 'Sorry, old boy,' and, placing the barrel to the horse's head, he squeezed the trigger.

In the silence of the afternoon heat, the gun blast sounded like a cannon exploding. Both Ben and Brad flinched as the weapon went off and the surviving five horses seemed to know exactly what had happened.

'I hate having to do that,' Reuben said as he returned to the wagon.

'Can't be helped,' Brad said. 'No way you can set a horse's broken leg.'

'I know, jus' seems like a waste.' Reuben sighed.

'I only hope there's no one near enough to have

heard the shot,' Ben said, looking at both men.

'Well, we'll soon find out,' Reuben said.

'We better git moving,' Brad said. 'Buzzards won't take long to see their supper.'

Brad mounted up and rode ahead as Reuben and Ben climbed aboard the wagon.

'Let's hope the five can manage,' Reuben said in a low voice. 'Giddup!' he shouted and cracked the long whip in the air over the horse's backs.

Hoofs dug in, some slipped in the soft sand, but slowly, the wagon was eased ahead as the remaining animals struggled to pull their heavy load.

Brad Morgan halted and turned in his saddle to watch their progress and make sure they could actually move. Satisfied they could, albeit slowly, he walked his horse on, keeping a close eye on the trail for any more holes and glancing ahead to make sure there were no riders.

Jed Greeley led his men along the northern trail. This was the route favoured in the past by Wells Fargo at the height of the gold rush. The trail was smooth and compacted and ran on level ground for as far as the eye could see.

The gang rode at a steady canter, sending up a great plume of dust behind them. The heat at this time of day was almost unbearable but on they rode.

Greeley called a halt as he surveyed the land ahead. He was looking for a marker that told him where to start heading south. It was a small cactus shaped like a man on one side of the trail. Greeley spotted it and grinned.

His men were busy taking a drink of water from their canteens and rolling a smoke as he waved them on, wordlessly. Hurriedly lighting their cigarettes, his men followed.

Reaching the cactus, Greeley rode on for another thirty feet before veering off the main trail onto a narrow path, made by critters making their way down to the river.

The Feather River wasn't in view yet, but Greeley knew that the path dropped down into a shallow valley and, once they crossed that and climbed up the other side, the river would appear from the crest of the hill.

His men followed blindly, they had both faith and trust in their leader as they carefully walked their mounts down the narrow path.

When Greeley reached the floor of the valley, he kicked his horse into a gallop and raced across the valley towards the other side, where he reined in again to make the gentle climb to the top of the hill.

He reached the summit in a matter of minutes and reined in; resting his hands on the pommel, he gazed down at the panorama laid out below him.

Even a hardened criminal such as he, a killer and robber, marvelled at the beautiful scenery which stretched towards the horizon.

Sunlight lit up the river and it sparkled like jewels, reflecting off the ripples in the water, painting an ever-changing picture. On this side of the river, the hills ranged in colour from dark brown to green and in places red where cactus flowers bloomed.

On the far side, the land was green with lush grass, a flood plain in the spring when the snows melted and the river became a raging torrent of angry water, escaping the confines of the river bank and spreading out across the fertile plain.

His men arrived beside him and halted their mounts; whether they took in the scene below them in the same way as Greeley, you would never know as no one spoke.

Greeley sat, gazing at the view for a full five minutes. His men, restless, began looking at each other, wondering what the delay was. Greeley studied the terrain carefully, noting the lower trail that led directly to Indian Bar. He knew there was only one way a wagon could get close enough to the river, which was the fork they'd left far behind them.

Looking from north to south, following the meandering river, Greeley knew they'd arrived before the wagon.

He smiled.

Then, without warning, Greeley kicked in his mount and began to descend the slope, heading for the river.

The gang's animals soon picked up the scent of the water below and the men struggled to slow them down. A lame animal here would mean its rider would have little chance of survival as each man doubted they'd get any help. They'd probably get a bullet the same as the horse.

There was no place for sentiment out in the wild.

Abe and Clancy saddled up. The horses were fresh and eager to go. Both men agreed to ride east and see if they could find the sheriff. They didn't know it, but it was the right decision.

Leaving town, they got curious looks from bystanders, townsfolk and strangers alike, as they cantered down Main Street, looking neither to the left or right and ignoring any calls from people they knew.

The more astute of the onlookers noticed that both men had full saddle-bags and a war bag, each hanging from the saddle pommel.

One man remarked, 'They sure ain't out for a pleasure ride.'

Reaching the town limits, Abe and Clancy kicked into a trot and followed the trail north-east.

Although both men were apprehensive as to the outcome of their foray, Abe felt more alive than he had in years.

'Hell,' Abe said, 'I jus' realized this is the first time I bin outa town in nigh on five years!'

'Well, not much call for it these days for me, either,' Clancy said. 'Nothing ever seems to happen hereabouts any more. Since the panners left and the two small mines closed down, all we had to deal with was the occasional drunk or separate a husband and wife afore they killed each other.'

Abe laughed. 'More excitement than I ever get.'

The two rode in silence, each scanning the trail ahead and the surrounding country, looking for anything unusual.

Then they heard a shot. The sound reverberated off the rock walls to their right, making pinpointing the direction it came from impossible.

Reining in, both men waited for more shots, but none came.

'What the hell d'you think that was all about?' Clancy asked.

'Reckon it was a pistol shot. But why? Your guess is as good as mine. Tell you one thing though, it weren't no gunfight,' Abe replied.

'How'd you reckon that?'

'Just the one shot. Could be a warning, a cry for help or putting down a lame animal. Maybe even shooting a wild critter,' Abe surmised.

Clancy absorbed these suggestions. 'Makes sense, I guess. Let's ride on and find out, eh?'

'Sure thing, Deputy.' Abe smiled and kicked in his mount to a trot.

It was no more than fifteen minutes before Abe spotted dust rising.

'Hold on, Clancy, there's someone ahead.' He pointed.

They were still too far away to make a proper identification and the shimmering heat haze obscured most things to a blur. By chance, they had reached the very part of the trail where it was closest to the river.

The launch site for the wagon!

Abe pointed to the small stretch of sand. 'There's some rocks there we can park ourselves behind and see who's approaching.'

Clancy nodded and they wheeled their horses around and headed for cover, both already drawing their Colt revolvers.

With sweat seeming to seep out of every pore in their bodies, the relentless heat from both the sun and that rising up from the sand, the men were drenched as they sat their horses and waited.

The tension was immense for both men: would it be the Greeley gang or merely a cowboy heading for Indian Bar? Clancy wiped sweat from his forehead, trying to keep his vision clear. Both men were finding it hard to control their horses so close to the rushing water of the Feather River.

It was almost twenty minutes later when a lone rider appeared on the trail in front of them. The heat haze still made it difficult to recognize the figure who had reined in and was beckoning someone behind him.

Within minutes, the wagon appeared. Still, Abe and Clancy did not show themselves, they had to make sure it wasn't Greeley and his gang. Any hurried move could prove fatal.

The horseman rode in closer and the sharp-eyed Clancy recognized the rider.

'Sheriff?' he called out, waving his hat high in the air.

'Clancy? What the—'

Both Clancy and Abe rode out onto the sandy beach towards the sheriff.

Reuben had reined in, and both he and Ben had their Winchesters trained on the unknown – to them – riders.

'It's OK,' the sheriff shouted to the Pinkerton men. 'It's my deputy.'

'Now would you mind telling me what the hell you two are doing out here?' Morgan asked.

It took Clancy ten minutes to explain the situation and after pondering, Morgan said, 'Seems to me they were in league.'

Reuben and Ben agreed. 'So, do we go on?' Ben said.

'We have to. There's no way these animals could pull this wagon back up that slope,' Reuben replied.

'Well, it's either the river or we head into Indian Bar and hole up there,' Morgan said.

'Wouldn't recommend goin' into town, Brad,' Abe spoke for the first time.

'Why's that, Abe?'

'Town's packed out, it ain't safe,' Abe said and took a swig from his canteen.

'Abe's right, Sheriff,' Clancy said. 'And where does the river come into all this?'

'We better get this wagon turned and backed into the water,' Reuben said, making up his mind on their course of action.

Clancy stared at them and then the sheriff.

'The wagon can be converted, apparently, into a boat of sorts,' the sheriff explained.

'Well, we got three more horses now,' Reuben piped up. 'If'n you three can rope on to the back of the wagon and tow, while I get the team to push us, we might get through this sand and deep enough into the river to get started.'

'Two extra guns won't go amiss, either,' Ben added. 'That's if you're willing to give us a hand,' he added.

'Hell, yes,' Clancy said immediately, 'but would you mind letting us in on what's going on?'

'Sheriff?' Reuben said.

Sheriff Brad Morgan told Abe and Clancy the full story and waited for their response.

Abe merely whistled. Clancy's mouth dropped open.

'You catching flies?' Morgan said to Clancy, who immediately closed his mouth.

'Well, I'm in,' Abe said.

'Me too,' Clancy added.

'Right, let's get started,' chimed in Reuben.

Jed Greeley reached the river first and dismounted, letting his horse drink its fill.

The rest of the gang soon arrived and followed suit, each man stretching and scratching and then reaching for their canteens as one by one they dismounted.

'Rest up a-whiles,' Greeley said. 'Then we lay our trap.'

The men were obviously puzzled. 'What trap is that, boss?' one of the men asked.

Greeley gave the man an icy stare and said, 'All in good time. All in good time.'

# CHAPTER THIRTEEN

Reuben and Ben fed and watered the depleted wagon team, before climbing aboard once more. Abe, Brad and Clancy tied their ropes to the rear of the wagon and secured them to their saddle pommels.

'On my mark,' shouted Reuben. He took a deep breath. 'Might be a good idea, Ben, if you was to grab the bridle of the lead horse, they don't like walking backwards.'

Ben agreed and jumped to the ground. 'OK, I'm ready,' he shouted.

'You boys ready?' Reuben called out.

The answer was a collective 'Yes'.

Reuben released the brake and shouted, 'OK, now!'

The three horsemen took the strain as Reuben eased back on the reins, encouraging the team to walk backwards. Ben, holding the lead horse's bridle, pulled hard in an effort to get them moving.

The wagon creaked and groaned as slowly, it

started to move. But it didn't go far. After reversing for a mere three feet, the rear wheels bogged down in the sand. Despite the efforts of the team and three riders, it wouldn't budge.

'OK,' Reuben shouted, 'rest up, we ain't going nowhere.'

Ben ran to the rear of the wagon to assess the situation.

'Damn! The wheel must be down two feet into the sand,' he advised Reuben.

Reuben joined to inspect the rear wheels.

'We'll have to dig a ramp and put the sacking on it to get some grip,' Reuben stated.

'An' move forwards again?' Brad asked.

Abe, the only one who stayed mounted, untied the rope and walked his horse to the river's edge. He watched the lazy current and wondered how deep it was. At this point, the river was no more than forty to fifty feet wide and Abe noticed the far bank was sheet rock, worn smooth by the river when it was in flood. The glare from the sun made it impossible to see any depth in the river, but Abe decided to find out.

He removed the saddle-bags and war bag, dropping them onto the sandy shoreline and then, unnoticed by the others, he walked his horse slowly forward, into the river. The animal made no objections, the water was cool and welcoming.

Already over ten feet from the bank, the water barely reached the horse's knees and Abe kept talking softly, rubbing the animal's crest as they progressed. They were about halfway across when the water reached stirrup level – deep enough, he thought, for the wagon to float. The current was mild and Abe felt no movement in their progress. He halted and turned in the saddle.

'Hey,' he called out.

The men stopped shovelling and turned to face the river.

'I got a better idea than reversing that there wagon.' Abe grinned.

He walked his horse on and it wasn't until he reached around three quarters of the way across that the current picked up and the horse lost its footing and started to swim for the far shore.

The horse didn't panic, even though this was probably the first time it had ever swum. After another twenty feet or so, the horse's hoofs hit the bottom again and it walked rather than swam to the rocky shoreline.

Abe took his hat off and gave a loud 'yeehaaa'.

Replacing his battered Stetson, he rubbed his mount's neck with both hands, the horse responded with a whinny and a stamping of hoofs as if it were proud of itself. Abe then walked the animal back across the river with no mishaps.

'I reckon once you get that wagon back on the trail, you back up away and take a gallop into the river. Your speed should stop the wheels sinking in. Once you reach the far bank, you can release the horses, leaving the wagon to float. What ya think?' Abe asked.

'Might work at that,' Reuben agreed. 'But first we gotta get the wagon outa this sand.'

111

The men worked with renewed vigour now they had another plan as, without anyone saying a word, they had all reached the conclusion there was no way the wagon could cross the short expanse of soft sand. Pretty soon Reuben and Ben were satisfied that the two grooves they'd dug in front of both rear wheels were sufficient and they grabbed the sacking to ram under each wheel.

'OK, you men push from the rear, let's get this wagon rolling!' yelled Reuben as he mounted up.

Reuben yelled 'giddup' and cracked the whip over the horse team's heads as the four men put their shoulders to the wagon.

The horses strained at the harness as the wagon very slowly moved forward. It stopped several times and Reuben's yelling and whip-cracking, as well as the four men pushing, gradually freed the wagon from the sand and back onto the trail. The four men who had been pushing were breathless and sweating profusely. Each of them was bent double, hands on knees, trying to get their breath back.

Clancy, being the youngest, was the first to recover. 'Hot damn, we made it,' was all he said.

'Pass me a canteen, young'un,' the sheriff said. 'I'm gettin' too old for this kinda stuff.'

'You are!' Abe said. 'I got five years'n more on you.'

Clancy returned with both their canteens. Ben, meanwhile, was with Reuben checking both rear wheels for damage.

'Well, we got away with that,' Ben said, wiping sweat from the back of his neck.

'Let's hope we get away with the crossing, too,' Reuben said as he handed a canteen to Ben.

'Hell, this water's warm.' He spat it out and walked down to the river's edge. Taking off his hat, he cupped his hands and splashed the cool, refreshing water on his face and neck. Seeing this, Abe, Brad and Clancy followed suit.

'Man, that sure feels better,' the sheriff said, wiping water from his eyes.

Reuben joined the group. 'OK, rest up a-whiles, then we'll make the crossing.'

Unbeknown to them, a late summer storm was brewing on the north-east edge of the Sierra Nevada mountains. Already, rain was lashing down in wind-blown torrents and running down in small streams to join the waters of the Feather River.

Further downstream, Greeley and his gang had made camp. The aroma of frying bacon and coffee filled the air. With look-outs posted, the men relaxed, waiting to see what the plan was.

Greeley helped himself to coffee and a plate of bacon and biscuits and, as usual, sat apart from his gang, facing the river.

Without being told, two of the men went off to relieve the lookouts so they could eat. Greeley was impressed. He'd chosen his men well.

He finished eating, went back to the campfire and refilled his mug with coffee, and called the men together.

113

Without preamble, Greeley started to speak.

'There's a wagon on its way downstream, heading for Sacramento,' he said. 'It's carrying gold bullion. Could be hundreds of thousands of dollars worth, could be millions. I aim to take it.'

His men seemed to be in a state of both shock and incredulity.

'A wagon?' one of the men said.

'A wagon,' Greeley replied. 'It's been converted, specially,' he added.

'How are we—' a man began before Greeley held up a hand to silence him.

'You may have been wonderin' what all that rope you got shared out between you was for,' Greeley said. 'We're gonna stretch it across the river and catch ourselves a big fish.' Greeley almost grinned at his own remark.

'The river hereabouts is quite narrow, maybe a hundred feet or so and the current ain't nothin' to worry about. So we secure the ropes on this bank, and two of you will ride your mounts across and secure it on the opposite bank.'

This last statement was greeted with stony silence. As one, the men turned to look at, what to them, was a vast expanse of water.

It was Cole who spoke up. 'Well, I for one will volunteer, hell, I'd fly across for a share in a million bucks!'

'I'll go with ya,' another man said.

'Suits me,' Cole said. 'When do we go—'

'How's a rope gonna stop a heavy wagon?' a voice

interrupted.

Greeley stood. 'This is no ordinary rope, it's ship's rope, much stronger than we use for a lasso. If'n it can keep a ship moored it'll stop a wagon.

'There's over 150 feet of rope here in three coils, we gotta tie 'em together an' tie 'em good. We loop it around the pommel of one horse and then secure it to another horse so that you both tow the rope.

'Me an' the boys will anchor it this end and you two find a suitable tree or rock to anchor it over there.' He pointed to the far riverbank which, as the men looked, seemed even further away.

Charlie the Knife sat on a rock and took his boots off.

'What you doin' that fer?' asked Cole.

'Man, these are hand-tooled boots. Cost me twenty dollars an' I ain't gonna ruin 'em in no goddamn water.' So saying, he tied them together and hung them around his neck.

Cole thought about this and took off his own boots. Charlie the Knife laughed.

'Hell, water'd improve them boots,' he said.

The rest of the men laughed too as they looked at Cole's cracked leather boots. Sole nearly worn through, heels run down at the backs and the pointed toes aimed skywards.

'They might not be hand-tooled,' Cole said, 'but they're all I got.'

'OK, let's cut the chit-chat and get these ropes tied.'

The three coils of rope were placed side by side

and Greeley knelt down and joined the first two coils together using a knot he'd been shown by the rope maker. When tension was applied, the knot would tighten further. He connected the third coil and then gave instructions to his men.

'Cole, do a double loop around your pommel, leave a ten foot length so Charlie can secure that end to his pommel. Now, when you hit deeper water, keep level so that both horses are taking the strain. The rope will get heavier as the water soaks into it.

'When you reach the far bank,' Greeley continued, 'use this.'

He held up a length of rope to which was attached a wooden pulley.

'Tie this to a tree trunk and pass the rope through the pulley. That way you can pull the rope taut. It's gonna be heavy so you best use one of the horses. Got that?'

'Sure thing, boss,' Cole said and took the pulley and stuffed it in his saddle-bag.

'The rest of you men form a line and feed the rope out. Got that?'

The men mumbled they understood and Greeley took one end of the rope and tied it round the base of a cottonwood, doubling a loop and securing it tightly. He tugged on the rope, making sure it didn't slip and, satisfied, walked to the water's edge to supervise the crossing.

Charlie and Cole mounted up and Greeley made sure the rope was secure on both pommels. He then checked the cinch straps of both animals, just to be on the safe side. The last thing he wanted was for the saddles to be pulled off. He didn't give a thought to either the men or the animals.

Satisfied that all was secure, he said, 'OK, take it steady, boys, and good luck.'

The last comment had Charlie and Cole taking a furtive look at each other. They hadn't figured on 'luck' playing a part in this.

'We all ready?' Reuben asked as he looked from man to man.

'Ready as we'll ever be,' Brad replied.

'OK, I figure this is what we do,' Reuben began. 'I can't force you three to go with us but would sure appreciate your help.'

'I reckon our horses can find their way back to Indian Bar,' Abe said.

'I'm with you, too,' Clancy said.

'Well, I sure ain't gonna ride back alone,' Brad said. 'You can count on me.'

The three men dismounted and took their saddle-bags, war bags and rifles from their horses and each in turn slapped the rumps of the animals, sending them off in the direction of Indian Bar.

Abe, Clancy and Brad clambered aboard the wagon and stowed their gear away – all except their rifles.

'OK. Let's do this.' Reuben climbed aboard the wagon, closely followed by Ben.

'You get ready to unhitch the team, Ben,' Reuben said.

Ben merely nodded.

Grabbing the reins in his left hand and the long, rawhide whip in his right, Reuben yelled a 'Yeehaa' as he cracked the whip and flicked the reins. The wagon lurched forward as the five-horse team galloped headlong towards the river. The momentum gained carried the team and wagon fifteen feet into the river, sending a huge plume of water into the air and soaked the men through.

Ben was keeping his eyes on the animals ahead, watched as the water level gradually rose and reached their bellies.

Within seconds two things happened at the same time: the wagon sank lower in the water and the horses were swimming, trying to keep their heads above water as the harness tried to pull them down.

Ben leaped from the driver's seat and edged his way forwards until he reached the lead animal, where he started to remove the harness the struggling horse. It wasn't easy, but he managed it and moved on to the other horses. It took ten minutes to free all the horses, who continued swimming to the opposite bank.

Using a wooden mallet, he released the cotter-pin holding the traces and watched as it floated for a while before the harnesses and chains pulled it under.

The wagon was now floating sideways downstream, moving slowly with the current.

'There's some paddles stored in that box to the rear of the wagon,' Reuben called out. 'We need to get straight on the river.'

Clancy clambered to the rear and brought out the paddles, and Abe and Brad immediately started to right the wagon. Ben meanwhile, was knocking out the pins holding the wheels in place. With the wheels not bearing any load, they were freed easily with a few hits from the mallet.

The wagon was now a boat – of sorts.

'Well, I'll be,' Brad commented. 'I never thought it would work!'

'I got news for you,' Reuben said, with a grin. 'Neither did we!'

'We still got a ways to go yet,' Ben cautioned. 'Let's not count our chickens.'

Ben lowered the tiller bar, which took some pressure off Abe and Brad's attempts at steering the wagon. Soon they were floating gently downstream with the current.

'This ain't bad at all,' Clancy remarked. 'Never been on a boat afore.'

'Sure get a different view out here,' Abe said.

'I reckon we got another hour of daylight,' Brad said, 'you ain't figurin' of staying out at night, are you?'

'Hell, no. We got an anchor, ain't safe to get too close to the riverbank in case we get stuck,' Reuben replied. 'We'll keep goin' for another thirty minutes, then park up.'

'Weigh anchor,' Ben said.

'What?'

'That's what you say, not "park up". And the left is

port, and the right, starboard.' Ben grinned.

'You turned into Columbus all of a sudden?' Reuben said.

'Who's he?'

'Never mind. Keep your eyes peeled along both banks, we don't want to get caught off guard.'

The wagon-cum-boat was remarkably stable and the current, not too strong, carried them along at a slightly faster rate than walking pace, which suited the five landlubbers.

The air was cooler over the water which made for a more comfortable journey.

The sun was lowering in the west and, with the intervening mountains, would disappear prematurely in this neck of the woods. Reuben made the decision to stop while there was enough light left to ensure they were moored safely.

Ben dropped the anchor and, as it hit the bottom of the river, the Conestoga halted mid-stream; the current kept it pointing in the right direction.

The men would take it in turns to keep a lookout, while Abe sorted through the war bag. Nothing hot, but even jerky and water was welcome.

The men ate in silence, keeping their attention on the river banks. Reuben didn't believe they were in any danger at the present moment. The darkness was their ally and unless the alleged robbers had a boat of some description, they were safe moored midstream.

Nevertheless, the look-outs changed every two hours and those not on watch fell into fitful sleep.

The storm in the north-east that had swept across Utah Territory was still heading due west. Torrential rain accompanied the thunder and lightning. Flash floods appeared as if by magic, engulfing gullies and then finding its way to the many small tributaries leading to the Feather River. A wall of water was racing south-west, carrying with it rocks and tree trunks as it gathered momentum.

# CHAPTER FOURTEEN

Cole and Charlie the Knife had reached mid-stream.

Greeley stood on the bank of the river, nervously chewing on a cigar. Although he would never show it, his stomach was in knots as he watched the progress of the two men. He wasn't worried about them, or their horses. He was worried in case they didn't make the far shore-line. If they failed, he had no back-up plan. The wagon had to be stopped.

With two men on the far bank, it would be a turkey shoot. Then, using the restraining rope, his men could tow the wagon to shore.

As he watched, he could see that the current, although sluggish, was carrying the men south. Not by much, but it was another worry for him. If they drifted too far south they'd run out of rope.

He relit his cigar and drew deeply on it.

Equally nervous, but for entirely different reasons, Cole and Charlie clung to their reins with white knuckled hands. The far bank didn't seem to be getting any closer and both men wondered if their respective mounts could actually make it to the other side.

By now, the rope must have trebled its weight as it absorbed water and for every foot forward, both horses were being dragged three feet south. Both Cole and Charlie had lost all feeling in their legs as the cold water seemed to seep into their very bones. If they didn't make landfall soon, they never would.

'Just starting the third coil, boss,' one of Greeley's men informed him.

Greeley merely grunted. He could see the whole caper falling apart. That didn't make him a happy man.

The men were still feeding out the rope, but it had slowed down the further the two riders went. Cole and Charlie were at least a hundred yards downstream by now but still their horses swam on.

The light was fading fast and Greeley knew that pretty soon it would be as black as all hell. He looked at the sky and could see no sign of the moon.

Then a yell caught his attention.

Cole's horse had found purchase. Although the riverbank was at least twenty, maybe thirty yards away, his horse was now walking on the bed of the river. Soon after that, Charlie's horse was doing the same.

The relief the men felt as, gradually, their freezing legs were released from the water was beyond belief.

'We made it, Charlie,' Cole said, a huge grin splitting his stubble-coated face.

Even their animals sparked up as they sensed dry land and an end to the coldness of the river.

From the far bank, Greeley watched as his two men reached dry land. He grimaced, which for Greeley passed as a smile. Now all they had to do was secure that end of the rope.

Cole dismounted, almost losing his balance as he felt nothing in his legs, it was as if they belonged to someone else. He clung to his horse, stamping his feet, trying to get the circulation going again.

Charlie remained in the saddle, he didn't want the animals dragged off by the heavy rope. He could feel his horse fighting against the rope that the current was trying to take with it.

Cole kept a hold of his horse's reins as he sank to the floor, pins and needles in both feet as the blood forced its way to them. It took another five minutes before he felt he could stand again. Reaching into the saddle-bag, he retrieved the rope and pulley and attached it to a stout tree, pulling hard on it to make sure it was secure.

'I better tie our horses to this tree,' Cole said to Charlie. 'We need them to take the strain. It's gonna be hard for the two of us to take the strain as we feed it through the pulley.'

Cole led his horse to the tree and tied the reins to it. Charlie heeled his mount closer and they managed to secure his horse too. He dismounted and felt the same sensations that Cole had experienced moments before.

'Jeez!' Charlie hopped from foot to foot. 'Gimme

a minute,' he told Cole.

Charlie rubbed his legs up and down and eventually the pain eased.

'OK,' Charlie said, 'let's get this done.'

Slowly, Charlie untied the rope from his pommel and, gripping with both hands, took the strain from his horse. Cole's horse whinnied and started to move to his right, but Cole held onto the saddle to still the animal.

'This is gonna be tricky,' Cole said. 'I'll hold the rope this end and you untie it from my pommel, but keep hold of that end, I don't think I can manage it on my own.'

'OK, ready?' Charlie wound the rope round his waist and moved towards Cole's horse.

Only Cole and his mount held the strain now, so Charlie quickly unwound the rope from Cole's horse.

The pull on the rope was far greater than either man had expected and they were nearly pulled off their feet.

'Get your end through the pulley,' Cole gasped.

Straining, Charlie edged nearer the tree, his boots slipping in the soft, damp earth, but he managed to reach the pulley and slide his end through it, holding it firmly to stop it slipping out again.

'OK, I got it,' Charlie said, 'let go of your end and grab hold with me.'

Cole let go and it took all of Charlie's strength to hold the rope steady until Cole grabbed at it and between them, they started to pull the rope through.

Straining every muscle in their body, they very slowly began to make headway.

Cole checked over his shoulder to see if the rope was clear of the water yet, but they still had some way to go.

Greeley chewed on his cigar; tension and sweat filled him as he watched the two men struggle with the rope.

'You three,' Greeley shouted, 'into the water as far as you can go and ease up that rope a ways, might make it easier over yonder.'

The three men, groaning, waded into the river until they were thigh high in water, as far as they dared go as none of them could swim.

'Right, pull and lift,' Greeley ordered.

The men did as they were told. All they thought of was the reward coming their way.

Gold did that to a man.


Three riderless horses arrived back in Indian Bar and made straight for the livery stable.

Their arrival had aroused no curious glances, every man jack in town was making his way to Latham's Palace and the delightful, desirable, Daisy Rae Mahoney.

Most of the men were slightly the worse for drink but there had been no major trouble in town that day, which was just as well, for the men the mayor had 'volunteered' to act as temporary deputies were among the drunken throng making their way to Latham's Palace.

Only one man was sober. Only one man was not going to see Daisy Rae that night.

It was Caleb Green, the livery owner, who put more store in horses than he did people.

He was taking a well-earned nap when the arrival of horses woke him up. Clambering out of his cot, he made his way through to the stable area.

'Well, well, what we got here?' he said out loud, rubbing the neck of one of the horses. He recognized all three. 'So Abe, Brad and Clancy are horseless,' he mused.

Although not privy to what was going on, Caleb was no fool. He'd sussed out that the only reason he'd been asked to make a secure compound for a wagon that never arrived must, in some way or other, involve gold.

Caleb knew there was little he could do apart from take care of the horses. With no law in town and the mayor a waste of time, Caleb hoped that the sheriff would return soon – with the wagon.


Distant thunder sounded and Sheriff Morgan, who was on lookout, waited for the lightning. It came, but it was as distant as the thunder.

Morgan counted the seconds between the thunder and the lightning. He counted forty. He wasn't sure if it was an old wives' tale or not, but it was said you can tell how far a storm was and, if the count grew, it was going away; if it got less, it was heading your way.

The thunder rumbled again.

This time the count only reached thirty.

Shee-it! Morgan thought. All we need!

Thunder cracked again, sounding like a hundred rifles going off at once. This time the count reached twenty-five, but the thunder was much louder and the rest of the men snapped awake.

'What the—?' Reuben sat bolt upright.

'Storm comin',' Brad stated the obvious. 'Getting closer, too.'

There was a noticeable change in the river. Even landlubbers like the five men on the wagon could tell the river was running faster, the wagon was rising and falling, too.

'What the hell do we do now?' Ben asked.

Reuben started to speak, but the thunder was so loud and went on for so long, whatever he said was whipped away by the wind and the clamouring of lightning.

There was sheet lightning in the distance, but forked lightning surrounded them. The crackle of electricity sent sparks flying skywards as the lightning struck ground.

Brad had long since stopped counting.

'Should we release the anchor?' Clancy spoke up.

Before anyone could answer, they heard a roar heading towards them. It wasn't thunder.

Straining their eyesight in the brief glimpses they got of the terrain, they saw a wall of water, maybe three or four feet high.

'Jesus! Cut that anchor free!' shouted Reuben. 'We gotta ride this out!'

Clancy was the first to react. He grabbed an axe and hacked at the anchor line. The wagon started to move slowly, but gathered momentum as the current took it. Ben grabbed the tiller and did his best to keep the wagon midstream; if they grounded now all would be lost.

The water surge hit them five minutes later. It swept over the wagon, soaking its occupants and the river visibly widened as the raging torrent rushed on.

'Is everyone OK?' Brad called out, wiping water from his eyes.

There was an assortment of coughs, gurgles and grunts that answered him so he knew they were alive at least.

Although the current was stronger, Ben managed to keep an even keel and, as the first surge passed, things got calmer. The thunder and lightning had moved south and now the rain came.

It came down in sheets, making it almost impossible to see more than a few yards ahead.

'Someone get up front and tell me if we start to head towards the bank,' shouted Ben. 'I can't see a blamed thing from here.'

The eerie blue-white light of the streaks of diminishing lightning lit up the terrain for a split second before darkness returned. Leaving them all virtually blind.

Cole and Charlie were battling with the rope as the first flash of lightning struck. They'd managed to pull in around twenty feet of rope, hoping that would be enough. It was impossible to tell in the darkness exactly where the rope in the river lay. They only prayed it was high enough to catch the wagon. Walking around and around the tree, they secured the rope and slumped to the ground, exhausted.

Now they all had to play the waiting game.

Rifles at the ready, the men with Greeley spread out on higher ground to get the best shot. Cole and Charlie settled on a flat rock by the side of the river and an eerie silence fell, to be shattered by a clap of thunder that seemed to make the ground shake and the men jump in shock.

'One thing I hate more than anything else is a thunderstorm,' Cole moaned.

'I hate rattlers,' Charlie replied.

'What?'

'I hate rattlers, they spook me out.' Charlie pulled out a cheroot and lit it.

'What in hell has that got to do with—'

Another clap of thunder, which seemed to be right over them, silenced Cole. Then the lightning came. It seemed to roll across the sky in a vast sheet of ice-white brilliance before disappearing as quickly as it had arrived.

Cole shivered and fished out a flask, took a deep swig before passing it to Charlie.

'Greeley finds out about this an' you're a dead man,' Charlie said as he took the flask.

'You ain't gonna tell 'im, are ya?'

'Heck, no.' Charlie grinned, feeling the rotgut warming him from the inside.

Then the rain came. It was raining so hard the drops were bouncing back six inches into the air from the stone slab the two men were lying on.

'That's all we need.' Cole sighed. 'My night couldn't get any worse.'

'Let's hope not,' Charlie replied.

The two men rose and ran to their horses to grab their slickers. But by then, they were soaked to the skin.

Jed Greeley sat beneath a hastily erected tarp. A campfire had been lit and coffee was brewing. The rest of his men were on lookout, soaking wet and cold.

From his lofty position, Jed could see a wide stretch of the river whenever lightning struck. If there was a moon, it was obscured by thick, black cloud. The brief flashes showed the river as a silver ribbon, meandering through the plain.

Nothing would pass here without him seeing it, he was sure of that.

# CHAPTER FIFTEEN

The rain stopped as suddenly as it had begun.

So far, Ben had managed, with the help of look-outs, to keep the wagon from crashing into the shore or getting grounded in shallow water.

The initial surge had passed them and the storm, travelling south, was moving at a greater speed than they were. The river slowed down and was almost calm again.

'Hell, that was scary,' Reuben said.

'Sure was,' Brad replied. 'I never did get the hang o' swimmin'.'

'My pa taught me,' Clancy said. 'Threw me in a pond an' said, "now swim!" '

'Well, ya did it,' Brad said.

'Damn near swallowed the whole pond, though.' Clancy laughed.

'How in hell are we gonna moor up now with no anchor?' Ben's question sobered the mood.

'Simple answer is, we can't,' Reuben said. 'We'll just have to keep moving 'til we reach Sacramento.'

'Hell! How long'll that take?' Clancy asked.

'Should be no more'n—' Reuben began, but a rumbling noise behind them stopped him mid-sentence.

It was a sound they all recognized.

'Jeez! Not again!' Ben cried out.

'Hang on tight, there's another surge comin',' Abe yelled as the rumble and roar grew louder.

The men all held on to whatever they could, but their eyes were staring upstream into the gloom, waiting for the first sighting.

Ben gripped the tiller so tightly his knuckles were white with the effort.

Then he saw the wave.

'Hell's teeth! It's bigger than the last one,' he yelled as the water under them seemed to get sucked back and the wagon hit the riverbed briefly with a spine-juddering jolt.

Abe lost his grip as the wagon surged up when the wave hit them. It washed over the wagon in an icy flow, sending Abe overboard. He was swept off his feet, cracking his head on the side of the wagon as he fell into the roiling water.

No one saw him go, the spray and the darkness engulfed all the men and Ben, struggling with the tiller, could only guess their position in the river.

There was much more debris battering the wagon; tree trunks were tossed around like matchsticks as the power of the water surged forwards, sweeping everything before it.

The wagon was tossed like a rag doll in the water,

turning 360 degrees at one point then moving sideways with the strong current. Nothing Ben did with the tiller seemed to make any difference and, as one, the men thought this was to be their end.

The roar of the water filled their ears and all the men could do was hold tight – and pray.


With the exception of Latham's Palace, Indian Bar was quiet.

The hotel itself was a blaze of light and the deafening roar of the revellers echoed through the empty streets.

Daisy Rae Mahoney was preparing for her second performance of the night and the overcrowded saloon was awash with beer, whiskey and drunken men all intent on a good time and to ogle the beautiful Daisy Rae.

They didn't care what she sang, they weren't interested in the dancers, they just wanted to stare at the woman of their dreams.

So loud was their cheering and whooping that the thunder outside wasn't even heard. The wind had picked up and began to whistle through the batwings, clearing some of the thick fog of smoke that filled the room.

On the southern outskirts of the town, people began to wake up as the storm raged overhead. Some of the shacks were only yards from the normally placid river. The surrounding grasslands were a profusion of colour as wildflowers bloomed in the hot summer months. An idyllic spot, but the inhabitants had experienced flash-floods before and some of the old-timers knew what to expect.

Packing up what possessions they could carry, people began to make for higher ground. The rain lashed down and small streams of running water hindered their progress as they climbed to the north of the town.

One public spirited old-timer made it to Latham's Palace to sound a warning, but his voice was unheard by many and ignored by most, so he gave up and joined the exodus to higher ground.

Hastily erected shelters soon went up to at least keep most of the rain off the huddled groups of people who sat and waited. There was nothing else they could do.

Although the storm was travelling south, the rain was unrelenting and soon the main street was a quagmire of mud, but the only action taken at Latham's Palace was to close the double doors behind the batwings.

Now that the thunder had passed over, an eerie silence filled the air as the sheltering townsfolk, now over a hundred yards from the river and at an elevation, thought they would be safe. Straining ears picked up a distant roar.

'It's comin',' one man shouted. 'It's comin'!'

The wall of water seemed to have lost no power as it continued its unstoppable rush south. Although too dark to see what was happening, the silhouettes of buildings suddenly began to disappear and the noise was deafening as tree trunks, rocks and assorted debris crashed into and demolished any-thing and everything in its path.

The main body of water passed by quickly and by what little light there was, people could see that the river had risen by at least twenty feet and widened by at least a hundred feet.

The rain began to ease off and, one by one, people began to emerge from their shelters and stand and stare at the devastation below.

Women were in tears as they slowly walked down the slopes towards the area their homes had once stood.

All that they saw was barren ground as if a huge plough had passed over.

What they didn't expect to see was a wheel-less wagon.

Jed Greeley was getting angry.

His plan seemed to be failing at every level. He hadn't counted on the weather. There was still no sign of the wagon, and his hopes of stopping it, killing the agents on board and taking control of it were fading fast.

Maybe the weather had caused them to change plans. Maybe they had to take shelter someplace and wait for daylight, which by his reckoning was only an hour or so away.

And, elsewhere, the thunder moved further south and the rain began to ease.

That's when he heard it.

At first Greeley couldn't figure out what the noise

was but, with dawn beginning to break, there was enough red-laced light to see what was barrelling downstream.

'Hell's teeth!' he whispered to himself before shouting, 'Flash flood! Get back!'

Two of his men reacted instantly and raced up the slope out of danger's way, another three stared open-mouthed for a while as they watched the wall of approaching water before scrambling to their feet in the nick of time.

Cole and Charlie had no such warning.

Lying face down on their flat rock, the two men were taken completely by surprise as a tangle of water, rocks and timber smashed into their bodies.

Cole was killed instantly as a rock smashed into his skull, smashing his head wide open as if it were a watermelon. His body slammed into Charlie and both were thrown into the river. It took Charlie a tad longer to die as his body was pummelled remorselessly, ripping the clothes and then skin from his body.

Greeley watched the macabre scene with no sign of emotion showing on his face at all. All he could think about was where the gold was.

At that point, the strain on the rope became too much as trees lodged on it. It snapped like a whip cracking, powerful enough to cut a man in two.

'Mount up,' Greeley ordered. 'That wagon's gotta be upstream someplace or stuck on the trail and I aim to find it!'

'What about Cole an' Charlie?' one of his men piped up.

'What about 'em? You wanna jump in the river and see if they're dead or alive?'

'Well, no.'

'Then shut up and mount up.' Greeley kicked his mount forward, his men sullenly following in his wake.

It was Clancy who came to first. Coughing and spluttering, ridding his lungs of water. He sat up and was mighty relieved the wagon was on dry land. Vowing he'd never set foot in a boat again.

Behind, he heard other coughs and groans as, one by one, Ben, Reuben and Sheriff Morgan all regained consciousness.

All four men had cuts and bruises and knew sure as hell there'd be black eyes to follow.

'I lost a dang tooth!' Ben muttered.

'You're lucky that's all you lost,' Reuben said.

Brad sat up, a knock on the side of his head was beginning to swell up and he wasn't sure if it was water or blood running down his face. He looked around him, seeing the other men were alive. Then realization dawned.

'Abe! Where's Abe?'

The four men searched around the wagon, which rested precariously on debris from the flash flood.

'No sign of him here,' Brad shouted from the river side of the wagon.

'He ain't here, either,' Ben called out.

'Damn!' Brad sank to his haunches, his head bowed. 'He must have been swept overboard when the wave hit us.'

'Sorry about your pal, Sheriff,' Reuben began, 'but we gotta move this gold, and pronto.'

'Yeah, you're right,' Brad replied.

By now they were surrounded by curious townsfolk who'd made their way down the slope to the river-bank.

The river was still raging, and uppermost in both Ben and Reuben's mind was there might be another flash flood. If that did occur, the wagon and its precious contents could well be lost forever.

The sheriff and his deputy were immediately recognized by the crowd.

'Sure good to see you back, Sheriff.' It was Caleb Green, the brawny liveryman who stepped forward. 'This the wagon I was expecting?'

'No, Caleb. This is the wagon no one was expecting,' Morgan said.

The sheriff saw the puzzled looks on the faces of the crowd, but didn't go on to explain.

'One of you raise Mr Morrison, tell him his presence is required right away,' the sheriff called out and immediately a man ran off to fetch the bank manager.

Reuben looked up. 'Who's Morrison?' he asked.

'The bank manager. I figure we need to get this gold into the bank's vault,' Morgan said.

At the mention of the word 'gold' there was a buzz of low conversation amongst the townsfolk.

'Quieten down, quieten down,' the sheriff ordered. 'We need your help to get this gold up to the bank safely and quickly.'

'We could form a chain,' one of the men said.

'We ain't gonna get another wagon anywhere near here,' another added.

Brad turned to Reuben. 'How much gold is there?'

Glancing briefly at Ben, who nodded, Reuben, who could see no point in secrecy any longer, answered, 'Five hundred ingots. Each one is stamped and numbered.'

A low whistle and intake of breath rose up from the crowd of onlookers as they heard this.

'Jeez!' Brad whistled.

The sun rose fully from behind the distant mountains to the east, revealing the full extent of the damage and chaos caused by the water. Broken planks, trees, rocks and debris from the interiors of the shattered shacks littered the scene. Women began to cry and men gritted their teeth.

Families had lost practically everything and uppermost in their minds was providing shelter for themselves as quickly as possible. So the prospect of wasting time transporting gold to the bank did not fill them with much enthusiasm.

At that point, the disgruntled bank manager arrived, his fine leather shoes coated in mud. He was not a happy soul.

'What's the meaning of this, Sheriff? Dragging me down here at this ungodly hour,' Morrison blustered.

'Hold your horses, Morrison,' the sheriff barked.

'It's Mr—' Morrison began.

'Shut up and listen.'

140

Brad brought the manager up to date and added, 'So you need to get your staff in and the vault ready, pronto! You got that?'

'I'll have to contact head office first,' Morrison said. 'I'm not sure I'm authorized to—'

'Mr Morrison. You will do as I order or I will commandeer the bank. Do I make myself clear?' Sheriff Morgan rested his hand on his sidearm. 'And you'll be in my jail before you can blink.'

Shocked at the sheriff's outburst, Morrison said indignantly, 'On what charge?'

'Obstructing the law,' Morgan replied.

'We'll see about that!' came the pompous reply.

Morgan drew his pistol and loosed off a shot into the air.

That stopped Morrison in his tracks and brought a shocked reaction from the gathered townsfolk.

'Deputy,' Brad said. 'Cuff that man and escort him to the jail.'

Clancy's mouth fell open. Then he smiled. Morrison was not the most popular man in town.

'Erm, I don't have any, Sheriff,' Clancy said.

Morgan pulled out a set of cuffs from his belt and tossed them to the young deputy.

'Never leave the office without 'em, Deputy. You never know when you might need 'em,' the sheriff admonished.

Clancy caught the cuffs and walked towards Morrison.

'OK, OK, I'll get the bank organized,' Morrison spluttered, his pride and dignity shattered.

'That's more like it,' the sheriff said.

Clancy looked disappointed.

'Now I need volunteers to help move this here gold,' Morgan said. 'I also need half a dozen men well-armed.'

This brought an air of consternation amongst the onlookers.

'You expectin' trouble, Sheriff?' a man asked.

Morgan hesitated. He didn't want to alarm the town or cause panic, so he said, 'Just a precaution, is all.'

'You reckon we're gonna run off with a gold bar?' A man laughed.

Morgan grinned too. 'Better to be safe than sorry,' was all he said.

'We need to get organized, Sheriff,' Reuben said.

'OK. Listen up. I suggest the women and children make their way to the meeting hall, the café will be open by now so food will be available. The rest of you men,' Morgan took a quick head count, 'all those with rifles, raise your hands.'

Five men raised their arms.

'OK, you five spread out along the line and keep your eyes peeled. Town's full o' strangers an' we don't want any, er, misunderstandings. Got that?'

The men nodded.

'Now there ain't enough of us to reach the bank in one go,' Morgan went on. 'Clancy, you get into town and see who you can rustle up. Tell them it's official business. But no strangers, got that?'

'Yes, sir, Sheriff.' Clancy ran up the slope to get more help.

'OK,' Morgan said. 'Let's do this!'

Jed Greeley led his men northwards, following the river as closely as possible.

'Keep your eyes peeled,' he yelled back. 'Looking for anything that might be a wagon, or part of one,' he added.

He'd had to slow to a walking pace to avoid crippling the horses on the scattered debris, which didn't do well for his already impatient manner.

As the sun's rays played across the terrain, steam began to rise from the tall grass on the far side of the river and soon formed misty fingers that intertwined in the grass, creating ephemeral scenes almost like a desert mirage.

Greeley noticed none of these things, his eyes fixed firmly on the assorted debris littering the river bank. His concentration was broken by a shout from the rear of the gang.

'Boss, something there, in the water!'

Greeley reined in and turned to look at the still-rushing water. 'What you see?' he asked.

'Looks like a wheel to me,' the man answered.

Greeley stared to where the man was pointing, but from his position, the sun's rays reflecting up from the water glared back at him, obscuring his view.

Dismounting, he walked back a few paces and, shielding his eyes, he caught sight of the object.

'That's a wheel all right,' he said. So they managed to launch it after all, he thought to himself.

Greeley considered the options: either the wagon

was resting at the bottom of the river and, unless there was a drought, which was unlikely, there was no way they would ever find it, or it had washed up someplace along the river, in which case they would find it.

Greeley was determined to find the gold. He'd never failed on any caper, and he didn't intend to start now. This robbery, unknown to his men, was his last. This was the one that would set him up for life and nothing, nothing would get in his way.

He walked back to his horse and heaved himself into the saddle. He flicked the reins once and set off at a walk. His men followed, Indian style and word-less.

# CHAPTER SIXTEEN

Reuben and Ben unlocked the false bottom of the wagon and exposed the gold bars. Neatly stacked, and spread evenly across the wagon floor.

There was an audible gasp from the onlookers as the sun's rays reflected off the bright yellow metal.

Sheriff Morgan had seen the look in people's eyes whenever gold was even mentioned. The looks he saw now were far more intense. There seemed to be a dangerous force at work whenever gold was involved. A few of the men even licked their lips at the sight of such wealth.

Morgan had never understood the power gold had over normally sane, reasonable men. He rested his hand on the butt of his Colt Peacemaker, not knowing what sort of lunacy might transpire.

The group of men were silent, doubtless thinking what they could do with just one of those bars of gold.

'OK. Listen up. Let's get this gold to the bank then we can all go eat!' The sheriff's voice seemed to break the spell and Ben lifted the first bar and passed it to Reuben.

The unloading began.

More men arrived, chased up by Clancy, and Sheriff Morgan paced the line of men as the gold made its way up the slope towards the bank.

Inside, Morrison was fussing around, intent on reasserting his authority in his own pompous way. He'd been cut to the quick by the sheriff, and he vowed he'd get even – when the time was right!

Reuben's place on the wagon was taken over by one of the townsfolk; Morgan thought it better that Reuben should, with himself and Clancy, monitor the transportation of the gold bars.

It was a slow job.

'Jeez! I never thought something so small could weigh so much,' was a comment repeated as each bar was passed from man to man.

After an hour, the men not used to manual labour were tiring, their arms feeling weak and weaker.

Progress slowed.

Morgan climbed up to Main Street and had an idea.

'Caleb,' he called to the liveryman. 'Can you get a wagon and team at this end of town so we can load the gold here and drive it to the bank?'

'I can sure try. Ground's soft, but I got six big horses, I'll get 'em hitched.'

Morgan then returned down the line and started weeding out the tired men. They were easy to spot as most of them were well known to the sheriff.

'OK, men, listen up. I've organized a wagon to be at this end of Main, so take a rest and as I call your name, you can go about your business.'

There was an audible sense of relief from the line gang, and the gold they were holding, they placed on the ground in front of them and took a well-earned rest.

Reuben and Clancy patrolled the line, just to be on the safe side, they didn't want any of the bars taking a hike.

Morgan had released eleven men from the line and called down the more able bodied men from Main Street to fill in the gaps. After twenty minutes, Caleb called to say he was in position.

'OK, let's get this done,' Morgan called out, and once again the gold bars began snaking up the slope.

The sun was slowly rising in the east and the strength of its heat beat down on the men's faces. The town was coming to life as Nature's alarm clock woke those up who had managed to sleep through the storm.

Every room in town was booked, some with four or five men sharing. Even the livery had a dozen men sleeping rough for a dollar a night.

More and more hungover men appeared on the streets, some heading home, others searching for something to eat.

Latham's Palace was closed, the mess inside would take all day to clear away. Latham wasn't bothered. He'd taken more money in two nights than he had over the last two months.

147

The café was full, the homeless families lingering over coffee for as long as they could get away with.

So five more riders entering Main Street to join the throng, caused no sense of alarm to anyone.

Jed Greeley couldn't believe his luck.

He sat open mouthed watching the gold, his gold, being loaded onto a flat back wagon in broad daylight.

'Well, boys,' Greeley said, and for the first time in living memory, he had a smile on his face, 'Lady Luck sure is on our side today.'

'Do we move in, boss?' one of men asked.

'Hell, no! We'll wait a-whiles. Watch 'em load up our gold for us,' Greeley said, his smile slightly unnerving his men.

Greeley dismounted, tied his horse to a hitch rail and sat on the edge of the boardwalk. He took out a cigar, struck a match on the wooden planks, lit up and inhaled deeply.

His men, bewildered, dismounted as well.

'Don't stand in a group,' Greeley barked. 'Just act natural.'

'How the hell we do that?' one man mumbled to himself.

The five men split up and watched as bar after bar was passed from hand to hand and loaded into the wagon.

'OK, hold up a while,' Caleb Green ordered. 'Don't want to overload and get stuck in this mud. Hold fire while I take this to the bank.'

The men gratefully rested.

Now is the time, Greeley thought. There's enough gold on that wagon to live like a king.

He stood and stubbed out his cigar, casually reaching for the Bowie sheathed on his belt. He took it out and, nodding to his men, walked to the front of the wagon as Caleb was about to board.

'We can do this the easy way, or the hard way,' Greeley said in a low voice as he pushed the eight-inch blade into Caleb's side, just enough to draw blood.

Caleb was no fool, not when it came to a knife being shoved into his side. He remained motionless.

'Here's what we do,' Greeley said. 'Nice and easy we get on the wagon together and we head down Main. Got that?'

Caleb nodded.

Greeley signalled his men to mount up.

'I got five shootists following. Any sign you give the game away an' a lot of innocent people are gonna die, starting with you. You got that, mister?'

Again, Caleb nodded.

'Good. Let's go.'

Sheriff Morgan had been looking down towards Ben and watched as the sunlight reflected off the river when he suddenly looked up towards Main Street just as the wagon set off.

Who the hell is up there with Caleb? Morgan knew what a stickler Caleb was. He hated anyone on his flatbed, always had.

Morgan began the climb to Main Street, the hairs on the back of his neck were standing on edge. As he neared, he saw five men on horseback and a riderless horse following.

'Clancy, get up here, now!' Morgan began to run but the slope was slippery, making going tough. Clancy, being a younger man, soon caught him up.

'What's wrong, Sheriff?' he asked.

'Keep it quiet, but I think that's the Greeley gang riding off with Caleb,' the sheriff answered. 'Go tell Ben and Reuben, get them to meet me in the livery an' make sure you tell 'em where it is. I want you to stay here and keep an eye on this gold. Got that?'

'But, Sheriff—'

'Don't argue with me, Deputy. That's an order!' Morgan gritted.

Clancy literally pouted and stomped back down the slope.

Morgan made it to Main Street and ran through the mud to get his horse from the livery; he knew it would be there, along with Abe and Clancy's.

By the time he'd saddled up, Ben and Reuben reached the livery.

'What makes you think it's the Greeley gang?' Ben asked as he and Reuben grabbed saddles.

'Ol' Caleb don't let no one ride his flatbed, and he's got company. There's also five men riding behind the wagon.'

'You gettin' a posse together?' Ben asked.

'An' leave all that gold at the mercy of anyone who grabs it? No, there ain't time. It's down to us. Sheriff's office first, pick up ammo, then we go to war, gentlemen.'

150

Morrison was standing outside the bank, waiting for the gold to arrive. He was a nervous man, but tried to hide it. He felt a great sense of responsibility and knew that if all went well, head office might reward him with a bigger bank in a bigger town, even a city if he was lucky.

If it was to go wrong, it would be the end of his career.

He saw the wagon coming towards him and stepped into the muddy street and raised an arm.

'Who's that?' Greeley asked Caleb.

'Bank manager,' Caleb replied.

'Well, he better step back.'

'I ain't about to run him down.'

Greeley, still holding the Bowie in his left hand, prodded Caleb's side harder. With his right hand he withdrew an Indian throwing knife.

Morrison, unaware of any danger, stood his ground, expecting Caleb to rein in so that the gold could be unloaded.

'You better move, banker man,' Greeley called out.

Morrison was confused, and that confusion cost him his life.

He stood staring at Caleb and the stranger sitting beside him and just as it dawned on him that something was wrong, Greeley threw the Indian knife with deadly accuracy.

Morrison remained standing stock still. He had

time to look down at his chest and see the hilt of the knife and a trail of blood run down his over-sized belly, before he fell, face forward into the mud.

Greeley grabbed the reins and flicked them hard on the team's backs, urging them on faster. He looked down at the bank manager's body as the wagon's wheels ran over his lifeless form, pushing it further into the mud.

As the animals picked up speed, the wagon became more unstable. In places, the mud was deeper than in others, causing the wagon to slip and slide. Caleb had the reins and he tried desperately to control the team but the wagon was alternately tugging them and then pushing them, and the animals were beginning to panic as their own footing was unsure.

The wagon suddenly leaned violently as the left side wheels hit a long patch of deep, soft mud, while the right were on firmer ground. This action pulled the horses left and Caleb fought with the reins to keep them right.

He failed.

The lead left horse stumbled, tried to regain its footing, but the weight of the wagon pushed onwards, its momentum forcing the animal to its knees as the wagon swerved left and then over-turned.

Caleb braced himself, Greeley jumped to the right and, at the last second, Caleb jumped clear to the left. He lay winded as the wagon rolled over him. The last sounds he heard was the screaming of the horses as they were dragged down.

Greeley was in the clear, his men rushed to his side but he waved them away. 'Get the gold,' he yelled like a maniac. 'Get the gold!'

Approaching the scene rapidly, Morgan, Ben and Reuben started shooting.

Surprised, Greeley and his men fell back behind the wagon and began returning fire.

The sheriff reined in, followed by Ben and Reuben, and continued to fire on the wagon.

Gold bars were littered across the street and the horses were thrashing in the mud, trying to get to their feet but the harnesses were holding them down.

There was a lull in the shooting as both sides waited for the other to make a move.

'We can't get 'em from here,' Morgan said, 'we need to get round the other side.'

'Me and Ben can dodge down that alley,' Reuben said, pointing to his right. 'Then circle round and attack them from the rear, if you keep us covered, Sheriff.'

Morgan was more than willing to do just that. He knew that, at his age, he was incapable of running around like a lunatic.

'OK. On the count of three. One – two – three!'

Reuben and Ben sprung up like cats and had reached the alley as Brad fired a volley of shots into the wagon. He hoped that some of the slugs found a way through the planking to do some damage. At least it was worth a try.

The gang didn't return fire straightaway, but when Brad stopped, they started. Already soaked to the skin, Brad, lying flat on the muddy street, was now showered with mud as bullets zinged over, in front of and by him.

He kept his head low, feeling mud oozing into one ear.

Brad knew that sooner, rather than later, one of the slugs would find its mark. Him.

Abruptly, the shots at him stopped and he heard rifle fire coming from the other side of the wagon. Brad breathed a sigh of relief as he knew Reuben and Ben had outflanked the gang. He raised his rifle and started shooting again.

The air was filled with smoke as the battle raged on. Greeley's men managed to keep both the sheriff and the two Pinkerton men at bay, but they knew that the longer the battle raged, the more likelihood it was that the townsfolk could well join in and they would be greatly outnumbered.

An impasse was reached. Greeley knew they had to get out, but he was loath to leave the gold. Crawling on his belly through the thick mud, he grabbed two bars of gold. 'Grab some gold, boys, an' let's get outa here.'

The power that the gold held over the men was stronger than the fear of getting shot. They scrambled through the mud, and each man grabbed two gold bars, it was as much as any man could handle. They stashed one bar in gun belts and coat pockets in order to leave one hand free to shoot.

Greeley made it to his horse; slugs were ricocheting all around him as Reuben and Ben kept up a fusillade of shots. Sheriff Morgan had Greeley in his sights and, taking careful aim, he squeezed the trigger of his Winchester.

The slug caught Greeley in the thigh and the man let out a snarled screech, more in anger than pain. It creased the muscle, taking a chunk of flesh from his leg, but Greeley still mounted up, firing at the sheriff as he pulled rein and dug his spurs harshly into the panicking animal.

Two of his men weren't so lucky.

One, more intent on the gold than the bullets, foolishly stood up, leaving himself exposed. A lucky slug ripped into the back of his head and it exploded in a crimson ball. The man stood erect for a few seconds, before slowly crumbling to the ground.

The second man had reached his horse and was mounting up when a bullet ripped into his back, throwing him into the mud, face down.

Meanwhile, Greeley was making good his escape. Firing his Colt randomly until he ran out of bullets, he reached the edge of town.

With Reuben and Ben pinning down the rest of the gang, Morgan saw his chance. He scrambled to his feet and made it to his horse. Mounting up, he set off in pursuit of the man who had escaped.

He was sure it was Greeley.

Pushing his horse as fast as he could, given the condition of the ground, Morgan tried to keep to the firmer parts of Main Street to give the animal purchase. He'd lost sight of Greeley, but there was only one way he could go. South.

Behind him, Morgan could hear the sharp cracks of rifle fire as the gun battle raged on.

Ben had circled to his right in an effort to trap the two remaining outlaws in crossfire. Coated in mud and sweating profusely, he reloaded the Winchester, glad that Morgan had had the foresight to bring extra ammunition. He held his fire, hoping that the two men pinned down hadn't seen him make his move. Sighting along the long barrel, his finger resting lightly on the trigger, and the stock pressed firmly into his right shoulder, Ben waited.

Reuben, meanwhile, kept firing, and the outlaws' attention was solely in his direction.

Silence suddenly descended as both sides weighed up their options.

'We gotta make a break for it,' one of the outlaws voiced. 'We stay here and they'll pick us off sure as eggs is eggs. We're on our own now.'

'OK. I'll give you cover.'

'I'll bring the horses over, and we'll ride!'

The man began crawling through the mud, heading for the tethered horses that remained. The animals were skittish. Ears pinned back and the whites of their eyes showing as the gunfire resumed once more.

Reaching the animals, he reached up to release the reins from the hitch rail, careful that the horse's hoofs didn't kick out at him. Holding one set of reins tightly, he pulled the horse round behind him as he released the other set of reins. He had no choice now but to stand in a crouched position, hoping at least one of the horses would shield him from the gunfire.

Ben's finger gently squeezed the trigger, aiming at the only part of the man he could see: his legs.

The bullet ripped into the man's knee, practically severing the leg. The scream the man uttered would fill Ben's brain for weeks to come. But it had to be done.

Even before the man hit the ground, a second man leaped onto one of the horses. He was still carrying a gold bar in one hand as he grabbed the reins and lit out.

Reuben saw him coming and, raising his rifle, let off one shot.

The rider, with both hands full, had no means of defending himself.

The shot from Ben's Winchester caught the man high up in the chest. He cart-wheeled over the back of the horse and landed on a pile of gold.

Dead.

'All clear,' Reuben called out.

Ben slowly rose, the mud on his back already drying as the sun beat down.

He walked over to the still moaning man he'd shot, his leg hanging off at a weird angle.

Feebly, the man tried to pull his sidearm. He almost succeeded until Ben fired a slug into the man's temple.

The pain in Greeley's thigh was excruciating. He could feel the blood running down his leg and every jolt of the horse sent a fresh wave of pain coursing through his body.

The only thing that kept him going was the two gold bars he'd managed to get away with. Even through his pain, he smiled grimly to himself. His excruciating revelry was brought to an end as he heard the sound of a bullet passing his head so close by that he heard the *whizz* as it passed him by. Turning in the saddle, ignoring the agony in his leg, he saw the rider behind him, gun raised and preparing to shoot again.

Greeley pulled his Colt out and began shooting wildly. At the speed both men were travelling, the likelihood of a hit was remote.

It was then that Greeley's horse went lame. The animal ground to a halt as it struggled on three legs.

Greeley cursed. 'Damn fool horse!'

He jumped to the ground, landing on his good leg as Sheriff Morgan reined in, grabbed his rifle and hit the ground.

Greeley fell as the pain in his left leg intensified when he tried to put weight on it.

'Just you an' me now, Greeley,' Morgan shouted. 'You're under arrest.'

Greeley laughed, sounding like a deep growl.

'Many have tried, lawman, an' they're all dead,' Greeley gritted. 'And now, so are you!'

He raised his Colt, but Morgan was quicker. The rifle spat flame as the slug caught Greeley's gun arm and the Colt flew through the air.

'I don't die that easy, Greeley,' Morgan said as he

walked towards the prone man.

But Greeley wasn't finished just yet. His left hand reached down to his boot and slowly pulled out his Bowie. He'd kill the man, if it was the last thing he'd do.

Morgan towered over the outlaw, rifle pointing straight at him. It was then Morgan realized he had no cuffs, having given them to Clancy. Damn!

Then he saw Greeley's lips part in an evil grin as he brought his left arm up, the sunlight glistening off a shiny object.

Morgan didn't hesitate.

He fired.

# EPILOGUE

Sheriff Morgan walked his horse back into Indian Bar, leading Greeley's horse, the outlaw roped to the saddle.

During the course of the rest of the day, the gold was collected and the vault of the bank locked.

The outlaws were laid in a row, a photographer already on the scene, photographing the corpses. Nothing the Easterners liked more than seeing dead outlaws in their newspapers.

Of the 500 bars of gold, only two were missing. Either stolen, or lost in the river. Morgan thought it a small price to pay.

Settled in his favourite rocker once more, he took out his pipe and sucked on it contentedly as if it were just another ordinary day in Indian Bar.

Indian Bar is a real place. A mecca for hikers and contains many varieties of wild flowers that are admired by visitors from all over America.

The rest is my imagination.